"Creeps li̶̶ ̶̶ ̶̶ ̶̶ g. He wouldn't h̶̶ ̶̶ ̶̶e and *not* stuck a̶̶ ̶̶u̶̶nd to see your reaction."

Shaun turned from the window and his eyes caught hers. "Monica, that snake definitely wasn't there when we arrived a few minutes ago."

A violent shiver passed over her entire body. She swallowed, trying to get hold of herself.

Shaun looked outside again. Monica's stalker had been only a few feet away. The stalker had been watching them—had been watching Monica. This was the kind of man he hated—someone who thought he had the right to play with others' lives. The frustration of dealing with men like this had made him quit the border patrol, had made him feel like a cop who couldn't hack it.

Well, he'd catch this man. And maybe it would heal what was broken inside him so he could do his job again.

Books by Camy Tang

Love Inspired Suspense

Deadly Intent
Formula for Danger
Stalker in the Shadows

CAMY TANG

writes romance with a kick of wasabi. Originally from Hawaii, she worked as a biologist for nine years, but now she writes full-time. She is a staff worker for her San Jose church youth group and leads a worship team for Sunday service. She also runs the Story Sensei fiction critique service, which specializes in book doctoring. On her blog, she gives away Christian novels every Monday and Thursday, and she ponders frivolous things like dumb dogs (namely hers), coffee-geek husbands (no resemblance to her own…), the writing journey, Asiana and anything else that comes to mind. Visit her website, www.camytang.com.

STALKER
IN THE
SHADOWS

CAMY TANG

Love Inspired

Recycling programs
for this product may
not exist in your area.

TM LOVE INSPIRED BOOKS

ISBN-13: 978-0-373-44475-5

STALKER IN THE SHADOWS

Copyright © 2012 by Camy Tang

www.LoveInspiredBooks.com

Printed in U.S.A.

Dear Reader,

Welcome to Love Inspired!

2012 is a very special year for us. It marks the fifteenth anniversary of Love Inspired Books. Hard to believe that fifteen years ago, we first began publishing our warm and wonderful inspirational romances.

Back in 1997, we offered readers three books a month. Since then we've expanded quite a bit! In addition to the heartwarming contemporary romances of Love Inspired, we have the exciting romantic suspenses of Love Inspired Suspense, and the adventurous historical romances of Love Inspired Historical. Whatever your reading preference, we've got fourteen books a month for you to choose from now!

Throughout the year we'll be celebrating in several different ways. Look for books by bestselling authors who've been writing for us since the beginning, stories by brand-new authors you won't want to miss, special miniseries in all three lines, reissues of top authors, and much, much more.

This is our way of thanking you for reading Love Inspired books. We know our uplifting stories of hope, faith and love touch your hearts as much as they touch ours.

Join us in celebrating fifteen amazing years of inspirational romance!

Blessings,

Melissa Endlich and Tina James

Senior Editors of Love Inspired Books

Much thanks to Danica Favorite
for making my stalker creepier, to Lisa Buffaloe
for your invaluable information on stalkers,
and Cathy Richmond for help with physical therapy
for stroke patients. You guys rock!

Thanks to my editor, Tina James,
for simply being stellar. A big hug to my agent,
Wendy Lawton, for praying for me.

This book is dedicated to my #1 Hawaii fan club,
Mom and Dad's friends.

* * *

But God is my King from long ago;
he brings salvation on the earth.
—*Psalms* 74:12

ONE

Someone was watching her.

Monica Grant glanced around the bustling central plaza in downtown Sonoma, California, and rubbed the back of her neck, but the ugly, prickly feeling wouldn't go away. She remembered the well-worn phrase from her Nancy Drew books—"the hair stood up on the back of her neck"—but she'd never realized how true it was. Until now.

She couldn't actually see anyone looking at her—there were tourists strolling around Sonoma City Hall and the fountain, cars driving slowly around the square, shoppers stepping in and out of the quaint shops. A few locals across the street noticed her looking at them and waved hello. She waved back with a smile, recognizing them as staff from a nearby restaurant. The Grant family's successful day spa, Joy Luck Life, had helped bring even more activity to the small tourist town, and all of her family was acquainted with most of the local business owners and staff.

But as she continued walking along the line of shops and historical buildings, the creepy feeling crawled up her shoulder blades. She whirled around suddenly, but didn't catch anyone in the act of staring at her, or ducking into a shop doorway to escape her notice.

It had been a silly thought, anyway. She wasn't a spy. She was probably imagining things.

She turned to enter Lorianne's Café, a popular new restaurant owned by one of her high school classmates, which served California fusion cuisine made exclusively with local produce. She thought the feeling of being watched would go away as soon as she entered the building, but an uncomfortable shaft of prickling shot down her spine. She turned to look out the restaurant's glass front doors, toward the green park area around Sonoma City Hall, but couldn't see anyone except a few tourists walking by.

"Monica Grant, are you stalking me?"

The voice, still betraying the slight Irish lilt of his homeland, made her turn. "Mr. O'Neill! I should say, *you're* stalking *me*."

Patrick O'Neill's light blue eyes creased deeply at the corners. "Seeing you at the Zoe International charity banquet last week wasn't enough. I had to get in more of your lovely company." He enfolded her in a hug that made her cheek rasp against his usual Hawaiian-print, button-down shirt. Quite a contrast to the tuxedo he'd worn at the annual dinner that Zoe International, an anti-human-slavery organization, had hosted to thank its donors.

"Are you here in Sonoma just for the day?" Monica asked. "Or are you staying overnight before you head back down to Marin?"

"I'm here for a few days, spending time with my new grandson."

"That's right, I heard about the new baby yesterday from Aunt Becca." At first Monica had been shocked because she'd thought the new baby was Shaun's son, but quickly realized her mistake—it was Brady's son, Shaun's nephew. She hoped Aunt Becca hadn't noticed her initial stunned reaction.

"What have you been up to in the seven whole days since

I've seen you?" He tugged at a silver lock of hair on his wide forehead. It brought back an image of Shaun doing the same gesture.

She forced her mind away from his eldest son. "I'm still taking care of Dad since he had his stroke."

"He's doing better? Last week, we were interrupted before I could ask you about him."

"He still needs a live-in nurse, but I'm also taking him to physical therapy several times a week, and he's gaining mobility back. He doesn't need me quite as much, which is good, because my sister Naomi announced her engagement six weeks ago. She's planning her wedding, so sometimes when she has to take off work at the spa, I fill in as manager for her."

"Will she still be manager when she marries?"

"No, she's going to start her own private massage therapy business in the city, closer to her future husband's office. We're trying to hire someone to take over when she leaves, but until then…" She had to stifle a small sigh. Because she still took care of her dad, filling in for Naomi stole precious free time that she didn't have. The spa needed to hire some-one soon.

"From nurse to manager." His blue eyes were more pierc-ing than his son's. "It doesn't sit with you well?"

His insight startled her. "I loved being an Emergency Room nurse," she said, "but I have to admit I don't regret quitting my job at Good Samaritan Hospital when Dad needed me. What I'd really like to do is run a free children's clinic for Sonoma and Napa counties."

Unlike Monica's father, Mr. O'Neill didn't roll his eyes at her. Instead, he nodded gravely. "Then you should do it, my girl. You only have one life to love."

His phrasing touched her on a deeper level, stirred up things she had left collecting on the bottom. She shifted uncomfortably, then changed gears, giving him a teasing look. "So who are you meeting for lunch? Yet another struggling hotel owner whose hotel you're going to buy and then turn into a raging success?"

"No, I'm just here having lunch with my son." He gestured behind him.

Brady, his second eldest son, lived only a few miles from Sonoma in Geyserville. Monica's gaze flickered over Mr. O'Neill's shoulder, past the hostess waiting patiently behind the desk, toward the restaurant's bar…and she froze.

Shaun O'Neill stared right back at her. Her breath stopped in her throat and seemed to hum there. She recognized the strange sensation, something she had only felt twice before in her life—at her first sight of a cherry red Lamborghini, and the very first time she'd met Shaun O'Neill, ten years ago at a Zoe International banquet.

Her heart started racing as he rose from his seat at the bar and walked toward them. His expression was unfathomable. Was he happy to see her? Indifferent? Something about the way he held his eyes made her think he felt the same rush of intensity she did.

No, she had to find a way to smother the electricity zinging through her veins. Shaun was a cop, and she would never, ever date anyone in law enforcement. In the E.R., she had seen what that profession did to the families left behind, had tried to heal the unhealable pain of losing a fine man to a criminal's gunshot. She knew her heart wouldn't be able to handle it.

She also knew she wouldn't be able to handle *him*.

As he approached, his scent wrapped around her—a thread of well-tooled leather, a hint of pine, a deep note of musk—a combination uniquely Shaun's. "Hi, Shaun." She gave a polite smile that hopefully masked the way he made her feel so… alive.

"Hi, Monica." The deep voice had a slight gravelly edge to it, promising danger and excitement. "It's been a long time."

"I didn't know you were back in Sonoma."

"I quit the border patrol," he said softly.

"What?" Surprised, she looked up at him and immediately drowned in the cerulean blue sea of his straightforward gaze. Shaun had always been aggressive with his stance, with his looks—and he was that way now, standing a little too close to her, staring a little too intently. "I…" She cleared her throat. "I thought you loved the border patrol. The last time we met, you were so enthusiastic about it."

"I'm back to spend time with my family. I'm thinking of applying for the Sonoma Police Department."

"Not as exciting as the border patrol," she remarked, looking for his reaction.

He shrugged.

How strange. He still had that bad-boy air about him, but there was something that reminded her of a wounded dog. No, a wolf. A wounded wolf. She wanted to reach out to him, to help him if she could.

Wounded wolves still bite. She had to remind herself that he wasn't her type. She had to stop now so she wouldn't go any deeper. She wouldn't submit herself to the kind of pain she'd seen in the Emergency Room. She shook off the memory of a cop's widow's shaking shoulders and forced her mind back to the present.

Then something invisible raking along her spine made her jerk. She turned to look out again through the glass of the restaurant doors but only saw the same view of Sonoma City Hall, made of local quarried stone that looked more flint-gray today under the overcast skies. Different tourists from the last time she'd looked walked around the grounds now.

She was being paranoid. She had to get a hold of herself. She turned back to Mr. O'Neill. "The last time we talked, you mentioned how you were going to sell the Fontana Hotel in Marin and do consulting work rather than buy another hotel. Do you know when that's going to happen?"

Mr. O'Neill smiled at her. "Does your question have anything to do with the rumors I heard that your father's going to expand the spa and add a hotel?"

Monica grinned. "Guilty as charged. I have a lunch appointment in a few minutes, but do you have time today to talk about possibly consulting for him?"

He gave her a sharp look. "Have you talked to Augustus about this yet?"

Heat like a sunburn crept up her neck. "Uh…Dad mentioned yesterday how he needed help now that he's actually decided to go forward with the hotel."

Mr. O'Neill smiled. "I do have time this afternoon." He turned to Shaun. "Did you want to come with me or pick me up later?"

"I'll come with you." His voice was light, but his blue eyes flickered to Monica.

She had to remind herself that she wanted to speak with his father, not with him. "Great. Thanks, Mr. O'Neill. Three o'clock at our house?"

"Sounds good. Who are you meeting for lunch, by the way?"

"It's a potential investor for my free children's clinic. Phillip Bromley."

Shaun's jaw suddenly tightened and his eyes became shards of ice. "The son of the CEO of Lowther Station Bank in San Francisco?"

She nodded. "His brother's a medical missionary in Kenya. I've known Phillip for a few months, but last week at the Zoe banquet, he expressed interest in my clinic and mentioned that his brother might be willing to donate his time to the clinic when he returns to the States this summer."

But Shaun was shaking his head. "You should stay away from Bromley."

"Shaun…" Mr. O'Neill said gently.

"Why?" Monica said. "Phillip has always been perfectly civil to me." Whereas Shaun's wildness seemed to exude from him, only barely restrained by his conservative white cotton shirt and jeans.

There was also anger underlying that wildness as he answered, "It's just a mask. It's not the real him."

A mask? Monica hadn't seen that at all, and she prided herself on being able to read people rather well. She didn't particularly *like* Phillip—there was something about his manner that seemed too self-focused and self-serving—but she hadn't detected anything deceptive during the times they spoke to each other.

"He's dangerous," Shaun growled. "You need to stay away from him."

Shaun's commanding tone grated down her spine, and she lifted her chin to glare at his set face. "How is he dangerous?"

Shaun's lips tightened briefly. "He just is. You don't know him."

"And you do?"

"Better than you do."

"Children," Mr. O'Neill said in a long-suffering voice, "play nice."

Monica backed down. Mr. O'Neill was right, she was being childish. The same fiery temper that got her into arguments with her dad was now picking fights with a man who only wanted to…what? Warn her? Protect her? She wasn't used to men like Shaun, whose life work was protecting people. Her ex-boyfriends had mostly been artists and playboys, who all seemed "soft" now compared with Shaun's solid presence.

She had to admit that his presence made her feel less

uneasy, less vulnerable to the eyes that might—or might not—be watching her. She couldn't stop herself from glancing outside again, but saw no one lurking or looking at her.

At that moment, her cell phone rang, and the caller ID said it was Phillip.

"I'll talk to you later," Mr. O'Neill said quickly, giving her a peck on the cheek before letting the hovering hostess seat him and Shaun at a table.

She answered the call. "Hi, Phillip." Were his ears burning because they'd been talking about him?

"Hi, Monica. I'm sorry, but there's an overturned construction truck here on highway 121. I'll be about twenty minutes late."

"No problem. I'll be waiting."

She had the hostess seat her at a table, but stopped when she saw it was right in the center of the large windows at the front of the restaurant. She glanced out at the tourists and pedestrians on the street. No one was even looking in her direction, but she felt as if a cold hand gripped her around the throat.

"Could I get a table near the back?" she asked, and the hostess nodded and seated her at a small table at the back of the restaurant.

However, it was close to where Shaun and his father were seated. She didn't want to request another change so she sat, but it was hard for her to keep her head averted with Shaun only a few feet away to her right.

At least the horrible feeling of being watched was gone. She spent a few minutes checking her email on her phone, but then the restaurant's owner and chef, Lorianne, approached her table with a long white florist's box and a huge grin on her face. "Hey, Monica. I happened to be up front just now when this was delivered for you." Excitement radiated from her bright eyes as she sat down across from her. "Who's it from? You didn't mention a new boyfriend when I talked to you a couple weeks ago."

"I still don't have a boyfriend. Your guess is as good as mine." Monica didn't look at Shaun, but could sense him glancing at her at Lorianne's words. Really, what business was it of his? She wished she weren't so close to their table.

"Ooh, a secret admirer," Lorianne said. "Well, as owner of this fine establishment, I am entitled to view any and all flowers delivered." She winked at Monica.

A part of her was flattered by the gift. Who wouldn't be? But another part of her was wary. Who gave flowers to a woman through a delivery and not personally? Then it occurred to her that maybe Phillip had them delivered in advance of their meeting. He had seemed a bit friendly last week at the Zoe banquet, but she'd been careful not to encourage anything more than a business relationship. She hoped he didn't misinterpret her body language.

Well, she knew who it *wasn't* from. She tried to angle her body away from Shaun as she lifted the lid. An odd cigarette smell made her eyes burn, and she blinked away sudden tears.

In the box, nestled among white tissue paper, lay a huge dead snake.

Monica gasped and dropped the box onto the table, making the silverware rattle.

"Oh, my gosh." Lorianne's eyes were huge.

The ugliness of the gift seemed to stifle her, and Monica fought to breathe. Who would send her something so hateful, so horrible?

"I'm so sorry," Lorianne said. "If I'd known…"

"Monica, are you all right?"

Shaun's voice cut through the shocked fog of her brain, and she managed to swallow, her eyes still riveted to the hideous carcass. Then she felt his fingers grasp her chin and turn her head away from the sight into his concerned face. The blue of his eyes calmed her a little.

His finger caressed her cheek. "Breathe. Are you all right?"

She swallowed again. "I'm fine." Her voice came out shaky.

"Who is this from?" Mr. O'Neill's outraged voice filtered through her consciousness.

She steeled herself, then pulled away from Shaun's hand and looked back at the box. A white envelope peeked out from behind a jagged fang in the open mouth. Shaun reached forward, but she moved faster to take it, not touching the snake. Her fingers trembled as she opened it and pulled out a thick, plain white notecard.

Monica,
Consider this a warning. Cease your efforts on your persistent plans. Your free children's clinic will never see the light of day. I will kill you if I must. My course is set, my determination sure. If you do not abandon your clinic, my vengeance upon you will be "As the snake late coil'd, who pours his length, And hurls at once his venom and his strength."

It was unsigned.

The menace and yet the poetry of the words frightened her. She began to shiver violently.

Who would do this? Why would anyone want to stop her free children's clinic?

"'The snake late coil'd.'" Shaun's voice was hushed and yet harsh at the same time as he read the note over her shoulder.

At the quote, his father jerked in surprise, his brow furrowed.

Monica's fear chilled as she took in Shaun's burning eyes and pale face. "What is it?"

"Could I see it, please?"

Monica handed the notecard to him.

He studied it with a frown, which deepened as he read.

"Shaun?" Mr. O'Neill asked. There was an urgent gravity and also a slight quaver to his voice.

Monica could see the note in Shaun's hands tremble slightly, and she realized his hands were shaking.

He glanced at his father, and some unspoken message passed between them. Mr. O'Neill turned whiter than the notepaper and swayed.

"Mr. O'Neill!" Lorianne rushed toward him and helped him to sit down in a chair.

"I'm fine." He waved her away, but his hand gripped the table edge tightly.

Monica turned to Shaun. "What's going on?"

His entire body had become taut like a bowstring. His eyes darted to hers, feral, fierce. Then he blinked, and a steely determination replaced the fleeting wildness.

"The man who wrote this letter killed my sister."

He shouldn't have said it in front of everyone that way, but the shock had ripped through him like a California breaker wave.

"Right this way…" The hostess's voice died away as she approached the back of the restaurant with two lunch customers and saw them all around Monica's table.

Lorianne immediately moved to block their view and spoke to her hostess in a low voice. The woman smiled at the couple and said, "If you'll follow me, we'll find you a different table."

They walked away, but Shaun could see that the restaurant was filling up with people coming in to eat lunch. He reached over Monica's shoulder and covered the box with the lid to hide the snake from view—hers as well as any of Lorianne's customers.

"You have to call the police," Mr. O'Neill told her.

Lorianne looked a little strained at the suggestion, but she nodded to Monica. "I remember what the delivery guy looked like—short, really thin, big nose. Brown hair. I'll talk to the hostess to see if she remembers, too." She moved away to intercept the woman as she was returning to the front desk after seating the couple at a different table by the window.

Shaun sat at a seat at the table while Monica pulled out her cell phone, but she dialed a different number than 9-1-1. He was about to ask who she was calling when she said, "Aunt Becca, I'm at Lorianne's Café. I need you to call Detective Carter and have him meet me here."

"Monica, what happened?" Shaun could hear her aunt's voice through the cell phone, sharp with concern.

"I got a threatening note." She opened her mouth as if she'd say more, but then rushed on without mentioning the snake. "He doesn't need to bring an officer with him. I don't want to make a fuss and chase away Lorianne's customers."

Her aunt said something briefly and then Monica hung up.

"So Becca's still dating Detective Carter?" Shaun's father said, trying to adopt a normal tone of voice, but Shaun could hear the reedy thread of stress behind his words.

Monica nodded. "She has his direct number so he'll be here sooner than if I'd called 9-1-1."

Her clear amber eyes found Shaun's, and he could read the question in them about what he'd said about his sister. "I'll tell you about it when the detective gets here," he promised.

She also called Phillip and canceled the lunch appointment. Shaun's jaw tightened as he faintly heard Bromley's voice. Something about an overturned truck. He was probably lying.

Detective Carter must have been nearby because he arrived at the restaurant within minutes. He pulled off his sunglasses as he entered the dining room, and his gray eyes were filled with concern as he saw Monica. "Are you all right?" he asked, his voice kind.

"I'm fine. You know Patrick and Shaun O'Neill, right?" She gestured to Shaun and his father, who were sitting at the table. Detective Carter seated himself in the remaining chair. Then she pushed the box toward him and handed him the notecard.

The detective's expression grew hard as he read the note, but it grew fierce when he lifted the lid and saw the snake. "Tell me what happened," he said.

Monica recited how someone had delivered the gift to the restaurant and Lorianne had carried it to her. "I'll talk to her later," he said. "You don't know who sent this?"

She shook her head, but her eyes darted to Shaun. "But Shaun mentioned something about his sister," she told the detective.

Shaun looked to his dad, whose lined face seemed to have aged a decade. "Tell them," Patrick said, his voice weak.

Shaun paused, staring at that hated notecard, gathering his thoughts. Finally he said, "Five years ago, my younger sister, Clare, moved from Sonoma to Los Angeles to work at one of Dad's hotels and to be closer to her boyfriend, Johnny. She had gotten her MBA the year before, and she was consulting for a free family planning clinic where Johnny was director, which was also down in L.A. But a couple months after moving, she was found dead in her apartment by her roommate."

He had to pause, to let the ache in the base of his throat ease so that he could continue. "It looked like suicide—drug overdose. But I knew my sister. She didn't use drugs. Her roommate said the same thing, and they hung out together a lot. Also, I had spoken to her on the phone the day before. We talked every week. She wasn't depressed, and she wouldn't have taken her life."

His father nodded slowly. "I spoke to her once or twice a week, too."

"When I was going through her things, I found postcards and letters that had been mailed to Clare during the two months before she moved to L.A. and also a few mailed to her L.A. apartment. They threatened her life if she didn't stop consulting for the family planning clinic."

He realized his hand had clenched into a fist, and he willed his fingers to relax. *Breathe. You're just telling the story.* Except it hadn't been just a story to him. It had been a surprising and hurtful discovery to make after burying his only sister. Clare had been the jewel of the family, especially after Mom had died. Losing his sister had shattered them all.

"Did she file incident reports?" Detective Carter asked.

"I don't know if she did for the notes she received in Sonoma," Shaun said. "I did find a report number in her notebook, but for an incident report she had filed in L.A."

The detective scribbled in his notebook. "I'll look into it."

"I confronted her roommate, Angela, about the notes," Shaun said. "Clare had confided in her about it all. Angela said that Clare had kept this secret from Dad and me and my brothers because we were all too protective of her and we wouldn't have let her move to L.A. if we'd known." Shaun fought back the wave of guilt. He had known how desperately Clare wanted to leave Sonoma, which at its heart was a small town despite the heavy tourist traffic. But Clare had been the only girl among four brothers, and their mom had died years ago, so they were naturally a bit overprotective of her. But maybe if they hadn't been, she might have felt she could confide in her family and Shaun could have protected her.

"Did the L.A. police look into her death?" Detective Carter asked. "They should have, if she filed an incident report for the notes."

"They couldn't conclusively prove it wasn't suicide," Shaun said. "Her boyfriend and roommate had alibis. Also, Angela told me that Johnny had been receiving threatening notes and other death threats for over a year from anti-abortion activists who opposed the family planning clinic, so when Clare first got the notes in Sonoma, she thought they were along the same lines. She also thought the notes would stop once she moved, but the stalker found her in L.A. and kept sending her letters and gifts."

At the word *gifts,* Monica shivered and her eyes slid to the white box resting in front of Detective Carter. Shaun wanted to comfort and protect her as he hadn't been able to do for his sister.

As he hadn't been able to do for any of the women in his life.

"Couldn't the L.A. police find anything?" Monica asked him.

"They focused on the anti-abortion activists angle, but I thought that the notes Johnny got were different from hers. His were violent death threats, but one of her notes quoted from *Don Juan* by Lord Byron—the same quote as that." He pointed to Monica's note.

Her eyes became wide and dark in her pale face. "So that's why it caught your attention."

When he'd read it, he'd felt a burning in his chest like red hot barbecue briquettes. "I recognized the quote because I had looked it up when I saw it in Clare's note. It was the only time he ever quoted from a poem. The LAPD even searched the database for any quote from Byron's poetry being used in any other stalker or murder cases, but they never found anything that tied to Clare's stalker." Until now.

Shaun shouldn't have let Clare go to L.A. He should have argued more with her. He should have been there for her rather than down south on the border patrol. She might have confided in him. He might have been able to do something about the stalker.

He happened to look up and he saw Monica's eyes on him. She seemed to see through the expression on his face, past the words he said to the words he didn't say, reading his thoughts. Her eyes and her face were filled with compassion, reaching out to him. It was as if she were trying to tell him that it hadn't been his fault.

Except she was wrong. It had been his fault. He was supposed to have protected Clare.

"How did the stalker know she was consulting for the family planning clinic?" Detective Carter asked.

Shaun shrugged. "Everyone knew. She didn't keep it a secret."

"But how would the stalker have known if she was still consulting for them or if she had stopped?" Monica asked.

He hadn't thought of that. "I don't know," Shaun said. The notes had become more and more threatening, but he hadn't considered how the stalker knew she hadn't stopped working on the clinic.

Detective Carter made notes in his notebook. "I'll look into that."

"What happened to the family planning clinic?"

"It never opened, but not because of the death threats or Clare's death. Funding eventually fell through."

"And I'm working on funding for my free children's clinic right now," Monica said. "What does this guy have against free clinics?"

"Maybe that's the connection," Shaun said. Clare's stalking had seemed so random, but maybe they'd found a clue that would lead them to the stalker. "We need to check all the other stalking cases involving women working for free clinics."

"I'll look into it," Detective Carter promised. He then turned to Monica. "Stalkers are rarely rational, and they can also be unpredictable. Be careful. Keep an eye out for suspicious cars, try to make sure you're not followed when you go home from work. Call me at the first sign of anything unusual."

Monica nodded, but they were interrupted by a bustling at the front of the restaurant as her aunt, Becca Itoh, hurried into the dining room. Several of the other customers looked up at the disturbance she created in her panic, but Detective Carter rose to his feet and gave Becca a hard, meaningful look and a subtle gesture with his hand. Becca's gaze flitted around the dining room, then she walked calmly to join them at their table.

"Are you all right?" She gave Monica a hug.

Monica's hand grasping her aunt's shoulder clenched once, then relaxed. "I'm fine."

While Monica explained what had happened, it gave Shaun an opportunity to study her. She tucked her long, wavy hair behind her ear when she concentrated on something, and her clear eyes seemed to glitter like golden gemstones, framed by her dark lashes.

When their gazes had met earlier, his attraction for her had hit him like a train wreck. It was still the same today as it was when they'd first met years ago. Then, there had been an ardent fire in her eyes, which she hid behind a cool demeanor. Holding him at arm's length, like he had Ebola or something.

Today, she'd again tried to be cool when he first came up to her, but for a moment during their brief conversation, before he'd angered her, he'd seen a flash of warmth in her amber eyes, a softening of her mouth. It somehow soothed him in a deep place inside.

He had been confused, so of course he ruined everything by getting into an argument with her about Phillip Bromley.

It was for the best. He would be stupid to get involved with a woman like Monica Grant. Any woman, actually. All the women in his life ended up dead.

He hadn't taken care of Clare well enough. He hadn't been able to save those illegal immigrants who had been killed at the border by the "coyote," a smuggler those people had hired to help them cross into the U.S.

He felt like he'd failed all the people in his life he was supposed to protect, and he wasn't about to let another one in.

She might end up dead, too.

But sitting here, looking at her, it was hard for him to remind himself that she was better off without him. As he studied the curves of her face, the color of her lips, he had to admit that she was even more magnetic than when he'd last seen her.

"Clare never found out who the stalker was?" Becca asked Shaun, drawing his attention from the glossy dark waves of Monica's hair.

"He never met her face-to-face. She kept trying to find out who he was so she could issue a restraining order against him. She tried backtracking the packages he sent her, but couldn't come up with any proof of who it was."

He glanced at Monica and resolved to speak privately to the detective about his suspicions. No need to alarm her, but he had to give the police everything he knew so this madman wouldn't slip away between their fingers. That frustration nagged and ate at him like an ulcer.

Although Clare was already gone, he had been driven to find her killer. If this were the same man, here was a chance for Shaun to catch him.

He hadn't yet turned in his application for the Sonoma Police Department. He hadn't quite understood why he'd been dragging his heels, but now he was glad because it gave him time to investigate Monica's letter-writer—assuming the stalker followed the same pattern as he did before.

The man had already taken his sister's life, and maybe others in the years since her death. He had to stop him from terrorizing any more young women.

He would find out who the man was. And this time, he wouldn't let him get away with harming Monica.

TWO

"We're not done with this conversation," Monica's dad said. "I think you should just lay aside the plans for this clinic for now."

Her father was regaining mobility and strength in his legs daily, but he still required her strength to help him out of the car. She steered him into his wheelchair because the physical therapy he had been doing would have tired his legs too much for him to use the walker comfortably.

"Dad, I'm almost fully funded." She set in place the temporary wooden ramp up the front steps of the house to the front door, grateful that she'd parked in the circular driveway right in front of the door so it was only a short trip from the car into the house. "The investors I have are committed to the project. I've already got a hospital director helping me write the business proposal. I've hired an accountant to help with the financials." She unlocked the front door and disabled the house alarm.

As she wheeled her father inside, he argued, "But no one has actually given money to the project yet except what you've put in yourself. There won't be any harm in dropping the project for now and picking it up again when the police catch this stalker."

"There's no guarantee the police will catch this man,"

Monica said. She wheeled him into the library. "When I do start up the project again, I'd have to start all over from the ground up, including drumming up investors. It's taken me three years to get to this point."

"Monica." Her father gripped her arm, and she stopped to look at him. His faded green eyes were earnest and calm, rather than sparking with temper like they usually were when they argued. "I know this sounds like I'm trying again to get you to drop this project and work as resident nurse at the spa instead. This isn't about that. You're in danger, and I don't want you hurt."

It was strange to see him like this, concerned and calm rather than fiery and argumentative. The two of them were too much alike, which was why they'd been arguing about this for the past year.

And the truth was, she was angry. She had always gotten along well with people, and men in particular, but she never let them control her. She thought back to the bickering with Shaun at the restaurant and how her independent spirit seemed to always clash with his stalwart opinions.

But this stalker was trying to control her in a darker way than Shaun's forcefulness or her father's arguments. In general, she didn't like anyone telling her what to do, but this wasn't a situation where she could go her own way and thumb her nose at whoever was trying to dominate her.

"I know, Dad," she said. "I still haven't decided what I'm going to do yet."

The sound of a car in the front driveway sent her to the window, and she saw her sister Rachel and her boyfriend, Edward, climb out of his truck. Last week, Edward, who owned a greenhouse business and often hired day laborers, had brought to Monica an injured boy whose parents hadn't been able to afford to send him to the Emergency Room.

Taking care of him had reminded her of how much this area needed affordable care for children.

"What are you two doing here?" Monica asked as Edward and Rachel entered the house. Rachel held a beat-up metal pot, and from it came the smell of something scrumptious that filled the house.

Rachel held the pot out to Monica. "This is from Julio's mother, as a thanks for patching her boy up last week. Tamales."

"I love tamales." Just the smell was making her mouth water. "Did you want some?"

Before they could answer, the sound of another car in the driveway made her remember that Mr. O'Neill was supposed to arrive to talk to Dad about his hotel plans. Before they even rang the doorbell, she opened the door with a welcoming smile to Shaun and his father. "Come on in. Dad's in the library, but I'm going to wheel him into the kitchen so we can enjoy some of these." She held out the pot of tamales. "Won't you join us?"

"I never turn down homemade tamales," Patrick O'Neill said.

"I'm afraid we just came to drop them by," Edward said. "Rachel and I need to get to the greenhouses to check up on the plants for her scar-reduction cream."

"Is yours the truck?" Shaun asked. "Our car is behind you on the circular driveway."

"I'll move my car," Monica said. It was easier for her to move forward on the circular driveway and clear the path for Edward's truck than force Shaun to maneuver backward around the curve of the driveway. She handed the tamales to Rachel. "Can you put these on the kitchen table and get Dad? He's in the library."

Monica headed out the front door. She nearly tripped over

the wooden ramp, which she'd left over the front steps. She nudged it to the side with her foot.

She slowed as she dug in her jeans pocket for her car keys. She had a hard time grabbing them, and when she did, she was already at the car. She reached for the door handle.

There was another dead snake dangling down over the driver's side window.

Shaun had been about to join his father and Augustus Grant in the kitchen when Monica's strangled shriek startled him. He raced out the front door.

She had dropped her car keys as she recoiled backward from her car, her face white. He followed her gaze and saw the snake, seemingly tossed carelessly onto the roof of her car, with the head arranged to rest against the closed driver's side window.

He reacted swiftly, racing to her and grabbing her none too gently by the shoulders. He propelled her toward the front door, his arm around her as he hustled her inside. She stumbled over the threshold, but he tightened his hold on her so she wouldn't fall.

He shoved her to one side of the door and slammed it shut. He peered out through the long, narrow diamond pane windows on either side of the front door, but couldn't see anything through the fuzzy glass. "I can't see anything," he muttered. "Do you have any other windows with a clear view of your car?"

Edward and Rachel, both standing at the foot of the stairs, turned toward them with shocked expressions. "What's going on?"

Monica sagged against the wall, her breath coming in gasps. She pointed to her right through the open doorway. "Dining room windows. You think *he's* out there now?"

Shaun hurried into the dining room and moved aside the

drapes. The large window gave a clear view of the entire front lawn of the house, including the orange tree grove on the other side of the neatly trimmed grass. No movement.

"Your stalker is outside?" Rachel asked. She and Monica had moved warily into the dining room also, while Edward moved to the other side of the window and peered outside.

"Creeps like stalkers enjoy watching. He wouldn't have put that there and not stuck around to see your reaction." Shaun turned from the window and his eyes caught hers. "Monica, that snake wasn't there when we arrived a few minutes ago."

A violent shiver passed over her entire body. She swallowed, trying to get hold of herself.

"What's going on?" Augustus Grant's voice called from the kitchen. There was another open doorway into the kitchen from the dining room, and Augustus had a clear view of where they stood on either side of the window.

"Rachel." Monica motioned to their father, and Rachel hurried to Augustus and Patrick, speaking in a low voice.

Shaun looked outside again. Her stalker had been only a few feet away. He'd been close enough to be able to place the snake on the car in the short minutes between the time Shaun had entered the house and when she went outside to move the car.

Shaun scanned the front lawn. There weren't many places the stalker could hide. There was a small group of trees to one side of the property, but the rest of the front lawn had open, serene landscaping with artfully placed black rocks and a few low shrubs that wouldn't hide more than a rabbit. On the far end of the lawn was a grove of orange trees. Had he been able to run from the orange grove to the driveway and back in only a few minutes, with no one seeing him from the house?

Then it occurred to Shaun that maybe the stalker had been crouched behind Monica's or Edward's car when Shaun drove up with his father. The man might have been only a few feet away. Shaun might have even heard him breathing if he'd been paying attention.

If he'd been that close when Shaun drove up, the man would have had time to plant the snake and then get to the orange grove in the few minutes before Monica exited the house to move the car.

"Do you have binoculars?" he asked.

Rachel ran to her father's library and returned with a pair. Shaun searched the orange trees on the far side of the front lawn.

The tiny figure of a man came into focus. Peering through binoculars directly at Shaun.

The man bolted away.

No. He wouldn't let him get away.

Shaun sprinted to the front door.

"Shaun!" Monica shouted. "It's too dangerous!"

His hand was on the doorknob. She was right. He didn't know if the stalker had a gun or not. He had to protect Monica, not run after the stalker.

His hand dropped from the doorknob, but the frustration sizzled in his brain, making buzzing appear on the edges of his vision.

The stalker had been watching them—had been watching Monica. This was the kind of man he hated—the ones who thought they had the right to play with others' lives. The ones who acted like God. The frustration of dealing with men like this had made him quit the border patrol, had made him feel like a cop who couldn't hack it.

Well, he'd catch this man. And maybe it would heal what was broken inside him so he could do his job again.

"Are you all right?" Rachel asked Monica.

Monica looked up from where she sat at the kitchen table.

Dad and Mr. O'Neill were in the library, finally having their discussion about the spa's expansion into a hotel, and Shaun was outside talking to Detective Carter about what he'd seen through the binoculars. Edward had left because of an emergency at the greenhouses, but Rachel had stayed with her sister.

"I think so." Her gaze fell on the pot of tamales, forgotten on the table. "Be sure to tell Julio's mother thanks."

"I will. Julio's doing great."

"He should have gone to the E.R., Rach. He's lucky that gash to his leg hadn't been worse."

"I know, but it was his father's call. And at least you looked at him rather than no one at all."

What kind of world was it when a man couldn't take his son to the hospital because he couldn't afford it? The frustration welled up in her, buzzing in her ears. "It's not right."

Rachel looked at her in confusion. "What?"

"This area needs adequate medical facilities especially for the migrant workers and the farmhands. If my free children's clinic had been up and running, Julio's father could have taken him there and not had to pay anything." How could she abandon her plans for the clinic?

Monica wasn't the headstrong, gutsy one—that was her sister Naomi. But she also wasn't the logical, gentle sister like Rachel. She was the emotional one, the one who always thought with her heart and relied on her instincts. Were her emotions only getting her in trouble now?

And it wasn't just her desire to help children like Julio that drove her. She knew that, deep in her heart of hearts, she wanted this clinic because it would make her feel like she had accomplished something, that she was more than just an E.R. nurse. She wanted to help more people. Dad's insistence that she become a resident nurse at the spa would be her agreeing to fade away to insignificance, and she couldn't willingly do that when she had a chance to really make a difference in someone's life. In lots of children's lives.

"I don't like hiding," Monica told her sister. "I don't like waiting around and giving this man permission to keep leaving dead snakes everywhere I turn. I don't like putting my life on hold while I wait for someone to capture him. Even though I know it's dangerous, I'd rather fight him off than *let him win.*"

"Is this clinic more important than your safety?"

"If I did stop work on this clinic, would you feel easy knowing this stalker was still out there, maybe still watching me?" Monica demanded. "Would you be okay knowing he would be out there terrorizing some other woman? At least while he's after me, there's a better chance he'll be caught by the police." Or by Shaun, she realized. She could already predict what he was going to do, and it wasn't apply to the Sonoma PD. Not yet.

"But this man might have killed Shaun's sister."

"But I'm not Shaun's sister, and since I already know what he's done before, I can be prepared."

"Prepared? How? He's leaving gruesome gifts, he was watching you…"

"I can't stop him from watching me." Monica couldn't suppress a shiver that raced through her. It made her feel slimy. "But I can be smart about all this. I can hire protection."

"Like a bodyguard?"

"I'd rather have a bodyguard than be afraid of what some lunatic is going to do to me. And I know just the person to ask."

THREE

The O'Neills stayed for dinner, although the conversation and atmosphere were a bit subdued after the events of the afternoon. Evita, the Grants' housekeeper and cook, whipped up a cheese soufflé which was apparently the Grant sisters' favorite dish, but it left Shaun feeling a bit unfulfilled. He didn't say anything since his father enjoyed the airy concoction.

After dinner, Patrick O'Neill and Augustus Grant headed into the library for further discussions about the spa hotel, and Monica caught Shaun's eye. She motioned toward the kitchen with her head.

Evita had gone home right after serving the dessert, a rich chocolate cake. Monica went to the refrigerator and pulled out a bag of tortillas. "Chicken quesadilla?" she asked him.

"Are you still hungry?"

"No, but I know you are."

Shaun's cheeks burned. "Uh… Thanks."

She turned on the heat under a cast-iron skillet on the stove. "So are you still going to apply to the Sonoma Police Department?"

He wasn't sure how to answer that, then decided to be honest. "Not yet." Then he fired back at her, "Are you going to abandon your plans for the clinic?"

She hesitated before dropping a thin stream of oil on the cast-iron skillet, and her chin firmed. "No."

He wasn't sure how to feel about that. On the one hand, it was safer for her if she stopped her plans so that the stalker wouldn't hurt her. On the other hand, her continuing her plans for the clinic would keep the stalker in Sonoma, would keep him near her. Would enable Shaun to catch the psycho.

"Are you sure?" he asked.

"I've thought it over." She lay a tortilla on the hot skillet. "I won't back down and be a victim. I won't let him think he can make some threats and people will obey him. This clinic is important."

"How does your family feel about that?"

"They're not happy. Dad's still trying to get me to stop." She shredded some cooked chicken breast onto the tortilla, then topped it with cheese and another tortilla.

"It's dangerous." He didn't want her putting herself in danger and he couldn't get himself to encourage her to make herself a target just so he could catch the stalker.

She gave him a significant glance. "That's where you come in."

"Me?"

"Since you haven't applied to the Sonoma PD yet, how about working for me as a bodyguard?"

Shaun stared hard at her. "You want me?"

"You can't do it?"

"Of course I can do it."

"So what's the problem?"

He hesitated, then finally said, "Following you day after day will take me away from my investigation into the stalker."

"I figured you'd be doing your own investigation," she said.

Shaun didn't admit that another problem would be being

near Monica day after day. She made him feel both comfortable to be around her, bantering like this, and yet on edge because he was so attracted to her. He didn't want that attraction distracting him. He didn't want any romance in his life, he didn't want any women in his life.

Monica flipped the quesadilla with a spatula, and it sizzled on the skillet. "Did you consider that since I'm the target, you being with me would draw the stalker out?"

"You being a target isn't something to take lightly."

"I'm not, but I also trust you to be able to protect me."

Her words kicked him in the gut, and he turned away from her to look out the kitchen window at the side yard.

Why did she trust him when he didn't even trust himself? He had failed to protect his sister. He'd failed the people who died at the coyote's hands in that accident down at the border—no, he couldn't think about it. If he thought about it, the guilt would burn in his stomach and he'd see their faces in front of his eyes. "I can't protect you," he said.

Her brow wrinkled. "Why not? You're a cop."

"I'm—I *was* border patrol. I'm not anything right now." He couldn't take on a job of protecting someone.

Monica's shoulders settled, but then she straightened. "Well, I guess I'll find someone else to help me catch him."

"What do you mean, catch him?" Shaun took a step closer.

"I don't intend to sit around and wait for him to hurt me." She slid the crispy quesadilla onto a plate. "I'm the perfect bait. If not you, then I'll just find someone else to keep me safe."

"How do you know you can trust me? What if I was a terrible cop?"

She smiled at him. "A terrible cop? You? You're a born protector—it practically oozes out of you. It's in the way you stand, the way you walk, the things you say. It probably runs in your family, since you were all so overprotective of Clare."

He felt like she'd ripped away a shield. She had sharper insight into him than anyone else he'd known.

She continued, "I think you and I could find this stalker a lot faster than the overworked Sonoma PD could. We've both got a lot at stake—my clinic, your sister's murder." She paused, then added, "I'm not going to be a victim."

There was that word again. He'd quit the border patrol because he'd seen too many victims he couldn't save.

But Shaun couldn't stand by and let Monica be bait. He understood how she didn't want to be a doormat and give in to this creep, and if she was going to try to stop the stalker, he wanted to help her. "Okay, I'll be your bodyguard."

She smiled and held out her hand. "Great."

He shook her hand, but the point of contact between their palms made a strange sort of energized languor move up his arm, then his shoulder, then through his torso. He felt relaxed and yet tense at the same time. He abruptly dropped her hand when he realized he'd held it for too long.

Monica blinked rapidly, as if waking up from a dream, then handed him the quesadilla. "You should eat this before it gets too cold."

She cut herself another small slice of chocolate cake before joining him at the kitchen breakfast table under the window.

"Let's talk about what we're going to do," she said. "My business proposal is almost completed and my accountant is finalizing the clinic's financial plan." She glanced out the window into the dark and then suddenly froze.

His skin prickled. "What is it?"

Her face had become pasty. "I…I don't know. I thought I saw something move."

He whipped his hand out and yanked the cord to drop the blinds. He twisted the plastic rod to lever the slats closed, then shot out of his chair and snapped the lights off.

Her face looked ghostly in the dark. He stood close behind

her and peered out through the slit where the blinds didn't quite cover the edge of the window.

He had to wait for his eyes to adjust. He saw low azalea bushes. Was one bush a bit oddly shaped or was it just his imagination?

And then the bush moved.

He hesitated a split second that seemed like forever. He hadn't chased the stalker earlier because he hadn't been sure if the man had a gun or not. He still didn't know.

But the frustration of not being able to capture his sister's killer burned in Shaun's gut. The stalker was so close—Shaun wasn't going to let this person get away again.

"Stay here," he ordered Monica, and he raced for the sliding glass door at the other end of the kitchen that opened into the backyard.

He didn't bother being quiet—he flicked the latch open and hauled the door open, leaping out onto the dark back porch and jumping down the steps before turning and heading for the side of the house.

He caught a flicker of movement to the left of his head and he flinched. Something hard and heavy struck him in the cheekbone and jaw.

He didn't remember falling to the ground. Pain spidered out from his cheekbone, aching and throbbing through his jaw while lights flashed in and out of his vision.

Then a voice, low and male, whispered, "You'll *never* catch me."

He heard a rustle like a leather jacket, and then a shadow passed before his eyes. He tried to make his hands grope for the man as he walked away, but his limbs weren't responding. The side gate creaked on its hinges as the stalker calmly walked away.

"Shaun!" Monica's voice was worried.

He rolled to the side, but it made the pain in his head pool to his right side and throb behind his eyes. His hands gripped the earth under him, his nails digging into the dirt. His arms were shaking but he managed to push and sit up. The world tilted and then he saw Monica's anxious face, blurry and beautiful.

"I told you to stay in the house," he growled.

"The house alarm is on," she said. "When you opened the door, I had to turn off the alarm before it started blaring. Then I heard something thud. Looks like it was your face."

"He could have still been here," Shaun said.

"I heard the gate close, so I knew he wasn't here," Monica said impatiently, trying to get a closer look at Shaun's face. "Can you see okay? How many fingers am I holding up?"

"Three." He tried to haul himself to his feet, but the pain in his head jumped a magnitude and he had to pause a moment on his knees, breathing hard, before the throbbing slowly lessened.

"Let's get you inside." Monica took his arm and helped him stagger into the kitchen.

He sat heavily in a chair at the table and let the room spin around him. When Monica turned on the lights, he squinted and covered his eyes with his hand.

"Sorry," she said, "but I need light to look at your face." She pulled his hand away and he felt her soft, cool fingers gently stroking his brow, his cheek.

"You'll have a giant bruise," she said, "but I think you'll be okay. No stitches, anyway."

Just a giant headache.

Her amber eyes clouded to mahogany. "Did you see anything?"

"Nothing. I ran out and he hit me."

"I saw a shovel lying near you."

"He stopped to speak to me." The words came out hard

through his teeth as he said, "'You'll never catch me.' That's what he said."

Her eyes narrowed. "That's arrogant of him."

"It means he's more likely to make a mistake. This isn't the first time he's done this."

"This is the third time he's come after me in two days." Monica got a towel and wet it with cold water. "How often did your sister get letters from him?"

"Every day or every other day."

"I don't see a guy like this waiting too long to start harassing me, do you?"

"No."

"So that means I can pinpoint when I might have met him."

"What do you mean?" Shaun winced as she pressed the towel to his throbbing cheek.

"The only people I've talked to about my free children's clinic are my family, whom I've told not to say anything, the potential investors, my hospital director friend who's helping me draft the business plan and the accountant I've hired. I'm thinking the stalker is one of the potential investors I talked to in the past few weeks."

"Do you remember who you've talked to?"

"I attended three large parties in the past two weeks to meet people and talk about the clinic. Before those parties, the last investor I talked to was over two months ago. So I think the stalker could be someone I spoke to at any of those three parties."

"What parties?"

"The Zoe International charity banquet last week—your dad was there. The annual Tosca bottle unveiling banquet a few days before that, and then two weeks ago, the Sonoma Businessmen's Association dinner."

"You went to all those?"

"I went in Dad's place. He doesn't like going to those

things, but I use them as opportunities to keep up relationships with other businesses and the Joy Luck Life Spa, and recently I've been sending out feelers for investors for my clinic."

"So your stalker might be someone you met at one of those events," Shaun said. He reached up to grab her hand and stop her ministrations to his face. Her skin felt silky under his rough fingers, and he didn't immediately let go, instead rubbing his thumb over a smooth knuckle.

What was he doing? He didn't need complications in his life. He dropped her hand and cleared his throat. "Do you think you can come up with a list of people you spoke to about the clinic?"

She was staring at her hand. She dropped the towel onto the kitchen table. "I think so."

"You can leave off anyone who already knew about your clinic before two weeks ago. I don't think this guy would have waited longer than two weeks to start following you."

"Did you ever investigate how he might have met your sister?"

"I tried, but none of us knew when she'd started receiving the letters, and since I'd been down in San Diego at the time, it was hard to find out where she'd gone and where she could have met her stalker."

"There's a chance he'd try to meet me face-to-face again, without me knowing he's my stalker. Do you think that's something he'd enjoy doing?"

"Definitely." His eyes narrowed as he studied her face, which had a calculating look. "What are you planning?"

"For the past several weeks, I'd been planning to give a party for about forty people. Some of them are already investors for the clinic, but some need a little more information before they commit."

"So you're thinking you'll go through with planning the

party? And you can invite some of the people you might have met in the past two weeks."

"I can't invite everyone I talked to, but I can certainly invite many of them."

"If the stalker keeps coming after you, we can figure out more clues about him and narrow down who he might be. I remember he wore a leather jacket or leather coat tonight. I could hear the leather rustling."

"That's a start."

"Where do you need to go this next week?" He may as well figure out a plan for protecting her even with her schedule.

"I have—" she began, but they were interrupted when his father entered the kitchen.

"Sorry to keep you waiting, Shaun…" His voice trailed away at the sight of him. "What happened to your face?"

"The stalker was here tonight," Monica said quickly. "He attacked Shaun."

"What?" Augustus Grant wheeled into the kitchen. His face was drawn with both worry and anger.

"We were just about to call Detective Carter," Monica said, giving Shaun a meaningful look.

He interpreted it easily—*Let's talk later.*

Yes, and in the meantime, he'd plan what he needed to do to keep her safe. Maybe he'd find this stalker and somehow find redemption for how he'd failed his only sister.

"Is this absolutely necessary?" Monica followed Shaun into the gym at the Rubart Towers Hotel in Sonoma, a hotel that used to belong to Shaun's father before he sold it to the Rubart hotel conglomerate.

"I would think you'd want to learn some self-defense moves." Shaun led her into a general purpose room at the back of the workout room, a large area with mirrors all around and soft mats on the floor.

"I took a self-defense class." She removed her sweatshirt, leaving her only in a T-shirt and workout capris that made her shiver in the air-conditioning.

"I'm going to teach you some jiujitsu moves that will help you in close quarters."

"Aren't you supposed to keep me from getting into that situation in the first place?"

She meant it as a joke, but to her surprise, he turned away from her. In the reflection from the mirrors, his expression was almost anguished.

Then he turned back to her and he was back to normal, his face serious and intense. "Let's get started."

He taught her a few types of arm bars, which she felt comfortable with since they didn't require extraordinary strength or quickness on her part. Then he moved to a guillotine hold, and she felt guilty causing him pain as she practiced the move over and over.

But more than the moves themselves, Shaun showed her that she wasn't a weakling. He gave her confidence in her ability to fight someone rather than just giving in. If the stalker attacked her, she wouldn't feel quite so vulnerable.

"This last move is a triangle choke hold," Shaun said. He explained the jiujitsu move, which involved her performing a choke hold with a triangle formed with her legs. "Now lay on your back and visualize to yourself that I'm the stalker, I'm trying to hurt you."

When she did, he angled himself on his hands and knees on top of her, and a rush of feeling passed through her to see his blue eyes so close, staring down at her.

A long moment passed where he simply looked at her. She couldn't look away, she was drowning in that cerulean sea.

She couldn't get herself to visualize the stalker, because

this was so obviously Shaun. His strength and capability made her feel protected and secure, even in this vulnerable position on the ground. He gave off the aura of protectiveness that made her believe he would never hurt her, he would never abandon her, he'd do anything to keep her safe.

Something about his blue gaze became less businesslike and more intense. Her breathing quickened, and she could smell his musk, the scent of a pine forest after the rain. His eyes flickered to her mouth, staring for a long moment, and then he lowered his head and kissed her.

His lips were softer than she would have expected from such a tough, masculine guy. His hand stroked the hair wisping out from her temple, his touch gentle. He kissed her with a kind of wonder and carefulness, as if he were holding a butterfly in his cupped hands. She felt cherished and honored.

Reason filtered through her mind slowly, but when it made itself known, she remembered that she couldn't be doing this. Shaun was a lawman. He'd always be in careers where he could protect people, putting himself in harm's way to save them, like he was doing with her.

She couldn't bear loving a man and sending him out to danger every single day, wondering if today was the day he wouldn't come home. She'd seen those women in the Emergency Room, she'd comforted them and been devastated by just the thought of their pain. She had vowed she wouldn't be one of them.

She planted her feet and thrust up hard with her entire torso, bucking him off her so she could roll away and jump to her feet. He had tumbled to his side with a look of surprise on his face, but now he took his time standing up, and he didn't look at her.

She had a hard time looking at him, too, although she tried to adopt a businesslike demeanor. "Not a triangle choke hold, but it'll get me away from the stalker so I can run for help."

"That's good," he said gruffly. He turned his back to her and walked to the corner of the room, where a basket of clean towels stood. He tossed one to her.

"Thanks." She dabbed at the sweat on her neck.

When he turned back to her, he was again stalwart and confident, but not as aggressive in his stance as he usually was. A haunted look floated in the back of his eyes, something that went deep. What was it? Did it have to do with his sister? No, he'd had that look even before finding out about the stalker and telling her about his sister. He hadn't had that look when she'd met him ten years ago, but it had been clouding his eyes ever since he had returned to Sonoma after quitting the border patrol. Did that have something to do with it? It made her want to help him heal from whatever had gripped his heart.

No. She couldn't get involved with him.

She gave him a false smile. "We're good, right?"

"What?"

"The k-kiss—" she had a hard time saying the word "—wasn't a big deal. Just the heat of the moment."

He seemed startled at first, then a look like relief relaxed his brow line. "Yeah. We're good."

The relief should have comforted her, but perversely, it created a buzz of irritation in her head. "Good." She turned away from him and headed out of the room.

As she picked up her purse from the gym locker, her cell phone rang. She answered it as she exited the women's locker room to meet Shaun near the gym entrance. "Hello?"

"Hi, Monica, it's Phillip Bromley. I hope I'm not calling at a bad time."

"Not at all. I'm at the gym at the Rubart Hotel."

"One of Patrick O'Neill's hotels, right? Before he sold it to the Rubart hotel conglomerate?"

"Yes, have you been here?"

"Last year. It's fantastic. Anyway, I'm calling to ask if we can reschedule our meeting."

"Sure." They decided on lunch the next day at Lorianne's Café again.

As they were talking, she reached the gym entrance, and when Shaun saw she was on the phone, he moved a short distance away so she could finish her conversation. When she hung up, he asked, "You have a lunch appointment tomorrow?"

"At Lorianne's Café. You'll come with me?"

"Yes. Who are you meeting?"

She hesitated before admitting, "Phillip Bromley."

His brow flattened. "I warned you to stay away from him."

"Why? What do you have against him?"

"It's complicated."

"So you want me to offend a potential investor for the clinic, and the only reason you're giving is, 'because I say so?' That's not going to cut it."

He glanced around. The main area of the hotel gym housed the treadmills and elliptical exercise machines, and they were almost all filled with people exercising since it was close to noon. He pulled her a little to the side.

He stared at the floor for a moment, his expression fierce. Then he said, "I think Phillip Bromley is the stalker."

FOUR

Monica couldn't believe it. She'd talked to Phillip numerous times. Although she had a feeling he had another agenda, she'd never gotten any hint that he was dangerous, or that he was lying about his interest in the clinic. She had always prided herself on how well she could read people. Had she been grossly wrong about him? "You need to explain."

He looked away, staring at some people exercising a few yards away. "I grew up with Phillip. We were classmates in a private school in San Francisco from first through twelfth grade. You get to know someone pretty well when you spend seven hours a day with him."

"Did Phillip know Clare, too?"

"Not in school. She went to a private girls' school in San Francisco, and his family lives in Sonoma, but they didn't become friends until after Clare got her MBA."

"So if they were friends up here in Sonoma, what happened when she moved to L.A.?"

"He followed her to L.A. only a few weeks later."

"That doesn't make him her stalker."

"I've never trusted him. He always seems to be hiding something."

Yes, she'd gotten that feeling, too, but that didn't make him a stalker hiding his secret, did it?

Shaun continued, "Clare didn't consider him a close friend, but they hung out in the same crowd of friends down in L.A., went to parties with the same group of people, that kind of thing."

"Why would he pose as an anonymous stalker if he was friends with your sister? He had access to her almost any time."

"She also had a boyfriend and a roommate. And the initial letters threatened to hurt her if she didn't stop work on the family planning clinic, but he didn't do anything physically against her—no attacks, just malicious letters. Clare's roommate said that sometimes Clare thought the guy was only full of hot air."

"So he only wanted to manipulate her, he didn't intend to hurt her?"

"Eventually he did intend to hurt her. The stalker's later letters were more threatening, when she continued to ignore him."

"But what made you think it was Phillip?"

"Clare's roommate said that my sister investigated a nasty gift the stalker sent her, a bottle of snake venom. She traced it to a shop on Haight-Ashbury where the stalker had bought it illegally for five thousand dollars. The person who sold it said the man buying the venom matched Phillip's height, weight, coloring, and he wore a black leather duster coat like one that Phillip owns."

"Did she ask him about it?"

"Her roommate said she confronted Phillip, who denied it. Clare believed him, but her roommate didn't. Neither do I."

"Did you see a photo? Video surveillance?"

Shaun's eyes slid away from her.

"So you don't have proof that it was Phillip who bought the snake venom."

"The salesperson positively identified—"

"Phillip isn't unusual-looking. Light brown hair, light brown eyes, medium height. And it's Haight-Ashbury—a black duster isn't even going to turn heads among the people who shop on that street. There are people there in wild costumes every day."

"I'm telling you, Phillip is the stalker. Every time I've talked to him, he acts like he's hiding something."

"Everyone is hiding something, but it doesn't mean they're hiding a double life as a stalker. I don't think what Phillip is hiding is very sinister. I think it's somehow more self-serving."

"How do you know this?"

"I'm good at reading people."

But now she wondered if she could really be entirely wrong. Was he more dangerous a person than she'd given him credit for? She had detected some attraction on Phillip's side, but that had happened with other men, and she never encouraged any unprofessional interest. It seemed Phillip wanted to get close to her for some reason of his own, perhaps because of her wealthy family and her father's lucrative business connections. "Do you have any solid proof about Phillip?"

He pressed his lips together.

"Don't you wonder if your bias about him from your school years might be clouding your judgment?"

Shaun shook his head. "He's a...he's slimy."

She could admit Phillip seemed a bit slimy, but she didn't think he would send dead snakes to her.

Still, he'd known she'd be at Lorianne's Café. But anyone watching her could have followed her to the restaurant, too. She wondered if Detective Carter had discovered who had delivered the gruesome florist's box.

She gave Shaun a hard look. "Phillip Bromley is an investor, and I can't simply cancel our appointment. It's unprofessional, which would reflect badly not just on me, but also on the clinic and my father."

His face sobered at the mention of her father.

"I've hired you to protect me, so you'll just have to protect me when I meet with Phillip. And who knows, maybe he'll reveal something to prove he's the stalker." She was sure Shaun would appreciate that if it happened.

He didn't answer at first. She could almost read his mind. His protective instinct was warring with his desire for answers.

"Fine," he said shortly. Then he leaned closer to her. "But you need to do exactly what I tell you. Otherwise you might as well fire me right now, because I won't be able to protect you."

He was too close to her. The memory of the kiss came back in a rush. She blinked to clear her thoughts and sidled away from him.

"Fine." She didn't look at him.

How ironic that Shaun thought Phillip was a threat when it was Shaun who seemed more dangerous.

Shaun watched the door to Lorianne's Café from where he stood next to Monica. So far, no Phillip, only a tourist taking photos of the square and a woman with a baby carriage.

Her scent wrapped around him, something exotic, which made him want to move closer to her. She was distracting him just when he couldn't be distracted.

He remembered the same scent during that moment at their teaching session in the hotel gym. He didn't know why he'd kissed her. There was something about her that made him want to be closer to her, to let her soothe something inside him. But he couldn't let anyone touch that pain and bitterness, he had to keep it to himself.

He was glad she'd laughed it off. It was better for both of them that she did. He wasn't good for any woman, although protecting her and finding the stalker might help him find some peace.

Movement by the door drew him out of his thoughts. He should have been paying attention.

Phillip Bromley entered in an expensive business suit, holding a bouquet of red roses. The sight of the flowers and their vivid color made Shaun's shoulders hunch and tighten like a bull pawing at the ground. Phillip had on a wide smile, and his eyes were fixed on Monica.

She met him with a polite smile. "Thank you, Phillip. You shouldn't have." Shaun thought she should have chucked the flowers at Phillip's head, but she did hold the bouquet in front of her like a thorny shield, preventing Phillip when he tried to move in to give her a hug in greeting.

Phillip then turned to Shaun, who stood closer to Monica's elbow than he knew he should. "Hi, Shaun. I saw your father last week at the Zoe banquet."

"Hi, Phillip."

"Are you meeting someone for lunch, too?" Phillip asked.

Shaun wanted to say no, to say that he'd been thinking of joining Phillip and Monica, but they had decided beforehand not to make it obvious he was watching over her.

"No, I'm not meeting anyone," Shaun said. "I'm just here to take a leisurely lunch."

Phillip gave a bland smile. "My mom went to the baby shower for your brother's wife. She mentioned that your sister-in-law was worried about you. Something tragic happened down near the border, she said."

His anger at Phillip for putting Shaun at a disadvantage warred with a flash of images of the drowning van.

"Every job has its stresses," Monica interjected. "Businessmen have their own types of stresses, while law enforcement has an entirely different set. More physical, those requiring strength of body and mind." She gave Phillip a bright smile, then shot Shaun a look that said, *Don't let him antagonize you.*

Phillip's neck had reddened at the mention of the "physical and mental strength." Shaun wondered if Monica had said that deliberately, to contrast Shaun's larger, more muscular frame to Phillip's rather pasty, thin body.

The thought made him not mind her stern look at him.

"Well, we should get on with our lunch appointment," Monica said. "It was nice chatting with you, Shaun." She led Phillip to a table near the back of the restaurant.

Monica had already spoken to the restaurant owner, her friend Lorianne, about Shaun being her secret bodyguard, so Lorianne had given him a small table next to Monica and Phillip where he could keep an eye on them and eavesdrop on their conversation.

Phillip pulled out the chair to Monica's right, about to sit down, but she placed the roses on the chair, preventing him. Her purse was on the seat to the left, so he awkwardly moved to the seat across from her.

"I hope you like roses," Phillip said.

"Oh. Certainly," she said carelessly.

A part of Shaun felt relief that she seemed to be making an effort not to encourage Phillip's Casanova moves. She hadn't mentioned that Phillip had a more than professional interest in her. Sitting only a few feet away, listening to their conversation, was harder than Shaun had expected it to be.

"I bought the roses because they remind me of the dress you wore to the Zoe banquet," Phillip said. "You looked amazing."

"Thank you," she said simply.

"It was the first time I'd gone to the banquet. Do you go every year?"

"Yes. Dad has contributed regularly to Zoe International, and they hold the banquet every year to thank their largest donors."

"Speaking of your father..." Phillip leaned in with a smile. "I heard a rumor that he was going to expand the Joy Luck Life Spa into a hotel. Is it true?"

"I'm afraid you'll have to ask him, since I don't usually work at the spa," Monica said with a neutral expression.

"That's right, you've been nursing him while planning this clinic." Shaun thought Phillip's eyes were a little too bright. "I'm so impressed you can do both."

"Nursing comes easily to me," she said lightly.

"I'm sure you're too modest."

"I assure you, I'm not. The clinic is what I'm most passionate about."

"You did seem very passionate when we spoke about it. Your passion makes you quite beautiful, did you know that?"

Shaun clenched his fists. The man's flirting was going to get out of line soon.

"Phillip, why don't we decide what we're going to order, and then we can discuss business?" Monica's tone was polite and sweet—not slamming the door in his face, but putting an end to the conversational thread.

She did it so smoothly, it made Shaun wonder if she had a lot of men hitting on her. Of all the Grant sisters, he'd always thought Monica the most beautiful. She had clear amber eyes framed by dark lashes, with a smokey look that reminded him of some fashion models, and her long, wavy hair was darker and glossier than her sisters' medium brown hair. Her mouth was a bit wide, but her smile lit up her heart-shaped face.

Not that he'd seen her smile often around him.

She was too beautiful for someone like him, who had so much ugliness inside of him. So many ugly memories of people he couldn't save.

A glint of sunlight off glass caught his eye. He turned to look out the large windows at the front of the restaurant and saw the same tourist from before taking a photo of the building.

Tourists taking pictures of the historic buildings in downtown Sonoma wasn't unusual, but the building the restaurant was in wasn't historic.

The man was about Phillip's height. Brown hair, medium-to-slender build. He didn't quite carry himself like a tourist—none of the casual sightseeing movements of the head, or the typical wandering pace as he circled the square. He was focused on this building, on this restaurant.

He took another picture.

Shaun got up, interrupting the waitress, who had just come to take his order. "I'll be right back."

Shaun exited the restaurant and glanced around quickly before crossing the street. The tourist was still there. It looked like he was studying the businesses around Lorianne's Café, as well, but he hadn't moved from his position on the sidewalk across from the restaurant.

Shaun tried not to hurry as he approached the man, but the tourist happened to glance in Shaun's direction. In a flash, he turned to walk away.

"Excuse me," Shaun called after him.

The man broke into a run.

Shaun sprinted after him, adrenaline pumping through his heart and his lungs. If this was the stalker, he wasn't about to let him get away, not when he was so close.

Shaun was taller and had a longer stride. He caught up to him and then threw himself at the man, tackling him into the grass alongside the sidewalk.

"Oomph!"

The man's camera went flying, and as Shaun wrestled the

man's hands behind his back, he winced a bit as he saw the camera land hard on the grass.

"Hey! My camera!" the man cried.

Shaun paused. Something about this didn't seem right. The man seemed more upset about his camera than being caught in the act of spying on Monica. "Who are you?" Shaun demanded.

"Chris Durant."

The man's voice was higher pitched than the stalker's had been, although he could have been disguising it. But something about the sniveling voice seemed too far off from the taunting whisper of a few nights ago.

"What were you doing?"

"Just taking pictures."

"Of Lorianne's Café?"

"There's no law against it."

"Except I saw you take dozens of shots. Why that building?"

Chris didn't respond immediately, so Shaun pressed against his two hands held behind his back. "Why that building?" he repeated.

"Hey, you're heavy, did you know that? Man, he said I might get chased but he didn't say it would be from a sumo wrestler," Chris complained.

"What? What are you talking about?"

"The guy who paid me."

Shaun's gut tensed. "Someone paid you?"

"This guy paid me five thousand dollars to stand outside that restaurant and just take pictures. Only of that building. He didn't even want the pictures I took. He just wanted me to stand out there."

Five thousand dollars? Who had that kind of money? "Who was it?"

"I don't know. He didn't exactly give me his name."

"What did he look like?"

"I dunno. Brown hair, brown eyes."

"When did this happen?"

"A few minutes before you came out of the restaurant."

Only a few minutes ago?

"The guy said someone might come out to question me, and to just stall," Chris said.

"Where did he go after he paid you?"

"Inside the restaurant."

Shaun snapped his head up and stared down the street at the restaurant. Where he'd left Monica alone. "Quick, what was he wearing?"

"A business suit. Dark gray or dark blue?"

Shaun jumped to his feet and pushed past a few tourists who had noticed him and Chris on the ground and had cautiously approached them. He didn't have time for explanations. He had to get back to the restaurant.

But he had a feeling Monica would be safe. The stalker hadn't paid Chris to take photos. He'd paid Chris to be a decoy, to lure out Shaun or anyone who might be helping Monica.

Shaun had been had.

FIVE

Monica didn't want to offend Phillip, but he was making her more and more uncomfortable.

But it wasn't because she thought he was the stalker. It was because Phillip's true agenda was revealing itself. He didn't really care about the free children's clinic. He was interested in *her*. Or specifically, her family.

She'd met so many men like him before, who saw the Grant sisters as a way into the family business or the family money or both. This was the agenda he'd been trying to hide the last time she talked to him.

She reached out with a swift hand to get the check even as he reached for it.

"No, let me get lunch," he said.

"Nonsense. I invited you to talk about the clinic." She also didn't want this lunch to seem more intimate between the two of them, which it would if he paid for her. She handed the waitress her credit card and the slim leather folder that held the bill.

"Well, I hope we can have many more lunches together." He rested his elbows on the table and leaned forward.

Phillip was much more aggressive than any other man who had expressed interest in her, and it was giving her a rather creepy feeling. Maybe he really was the stalker? He seemed to have the same dogged persistence.

She leaned back in her chair to get as much distance between them as possible. "I hope you'll consider investing in the clinic."

"I think it would be great to work with you on just about any business venture." His smile didn't quite meet his brown eyes.

Business venture? Did he want in on Dad's hotel scheme? Was that his game plan—woo the only unattached daughter to become chums with Augustus Grant? The thought made her shiver with distaste.

Unfortunately, he noticed. "Are you cold? Why don't you take my jacket—"

"No." She stopped him before he could remove his dark gray business suit jacket. "I'm fine. I'm leaving soon, anyway."

"Oh, I was hoping we'd have time for a coffee at that new Italian espresso bar down the street."

Much as she loved Captain Caffeine's Espresso, Monica wasn't about to encourage Phillip's attentions. "I'm sorry, but I'm still taking care of my dad. I need to get home."

"Oh, of course. He had a stroke, right? He's, uh…doing all right?"

"He's getting better every day."

"Great, great." There was that smile again that didn't reach his eyes.

As Monica signed the credit card receipt, she realized she understood why Shaun didn't like Phillip. He was ingenuine, a trait that Shaun must hate. Shaun was so straightforward, so blunt and honest.

She wondered where he went. He'd dashed out earlier, but he hadn't returned to his seat. In fact, the wait staff had cleaned up and sat two young businesswomen at his table.

But even though she couldn't see him, she knew he was still looking out for her somewhere in the restaurant.

She rose, and Phillip stood as well. "I'll walk you to your car," he said.

"There's no need."

"I never let a lady walk to her car alone." His attempt to be gentlemanly sounded false to her ears. Was it because he was the stalker or because he was trying to get into her good graces? Her gut instinct told her it was the latter.

But what good was her gut instinct? She'd apparently met the stalker at some point in the past few weeks and didn't even pick up on the fact that he was displeased with her work on a free children's clinic.

No way was she letting Phillip walk her to her car. She'd never be able to get him to walk away before watching her open her car door, not without seeming rude or strange.

She was trying to come up with an excuse when they were interrupted by the waitress. "Miss Grant, Lorianne asks for you to please wait to speak to her. She's a bit busy right now, but she says she'll have a free moment in a few minutes. If you'll wait near the bar?"

Monica waved goodbye to Phillip and once he was gone, gave the roses to the hostesses and sat at the glossy oak bar, ordering a glass of mineral water. In a few seconds, Shaun sat next to her.

"Did you arrange for Lorianne's message?" she asked.

"You looked like you needed help pulling the leech off you."

Leech was a good way to put it. She felt slimy like Phillip *had* been a leech stuck to her skin.

"I don't think he's the stalker—" she said.

At the same time, he said, "I think he's the stalker."

They stared at each other. A warm prickling traveled up

and down Monica's arm, and she looked away from him. "Why do you think he's the stalker?"

Shaun told her about the man in the dark gray or dark blue business suit who had paid Chris to take photos of the building. "He did it to lure me out, but I caught the guy pretty quick and hurried back in here before you'd even been served your basket of bread."

"Where were you? I didn't see you."

He grinned at her, his teeth white. "I borrowed an apron from one of Lorianne's busboys and posed as one of them. But I didn't work near your table, so Phillip didn't see me."

"That was nice of the busboy."

"He, er, didn't know. Lorianne said it was okay, though. Plus it's so busy back there right now, I could have taken the apron and no one would have noticed."

"So why do you think the stalker is Phillip? There must be lots of men in dark gray business suits in the restaurant."

"Actually, there were only four, and only Phillip had brown hair."

"How about dark blue business suits?"

He hesitated. "There were three."

"Any with brown hair?"

"All of them," he admitted. "But doesn't it seem highly co-incidental that the stalker paid Chris and then came into the restaurant, and the timing matches when Phillip arrived?"

"But Phillip had roses with him."

Shaun shook his head. "I spoke to the hostesses. Phillip had the roses delivered to the restaurant and picked them up from the hostess desk just before going into the dining room."

Could it be? Had her instincts been so totally wrong about Phillip?

"You mentioned how busy it was in back," she said. "Couldn't the stalker have gotten rid of his jacket and blended in with the wait staff?"

Shaun's brows drew together. Finally he said, "You're right, he could have, at least for a little while. No one questioned me working as a busboy until after twenty minutes."

"I just spent an entire hour with Phillip. He came on pretty strong, but I think that he's interested in my family. He's trying to hide it and pretend he's interested in me."

"Your family? You mean the spa?"

"He asked me about the hotel. He heard the rumor somewhere."

Shaun's expression was puzzled. "But he's a bank VP. What would he want with a hotel?"

"Investment?"

"Maybe." He thought a moment. "Dad isn't friendly with the Bromleys. He's polite to them in public, but he won't interact with them otherwise. He doesn't like how Phillip's father treated some of his servants in his home, and when he talked to Mr. Bromley about it, apparently they got into an argument. Dad said he wouldn't be friends with anyone who didn't give people basic respect."

"I didn't know that about the Bromleys, or your father." No wonder there was so much animosity between Shaun and Phillip. If Phillip was anything like his father, Shaun would despise him for his lack of human decency. She could also see how Mr. Bromley's behavior would trigger Mr. O'Neill's sense of justice. His hotels were famous for a low staff turnaround because they were treated so well by management and didn't want to leave.

"Monica." Lorianne's voice behind them sounded breathless. "I'm glad you're still here. I needed to talk to you." The chef, looking frazzled, strode through the doorway to the kitchen and headed their way.

"You must be busy," Monica said. "I can call you later if you want."

"No, I wanted to tell you now so you'll stick around for another hour." Lorianne wiped her flushed neck with a handkerchief, which she shoved into a back pocket. "Wow, we were busier than normal today, or else I would have remembered earlier. I could have told Shaun to tell you when he asked to borrow a busboy's apron." She winked at him.

"Much appreciated," he said.

"I called Detective Carter this morning," Lorianne said. "I didn't remember at the time, but I recognized that snake in the florist's box."

"You did?" Monica grimaced at the flash of memory. "Where in the world did you see a dead snake before?"

"It's actually a species of snake used in unusual cuisine," the chef said triumphantly. "I recognized the markings on the skin. I have a friend—another chef—who's really into that stuff."

"So it wasn't just caught out in the wild or bought from a pet store?"

"Nope. In fact, it was probably bought freshly killed for cooking."

"You can actually buy them for eating?"

"That's why I wanted you to stick around. I'm going to be busy for another hour at least, but when I'm free, I wanted you to come back to my office. We can call the store owner who sells those things. I've ordered some hard-to-find Asian herbs from him before because he specializes in unusual ingredients, although he tends to be really pricy."

Of course Lorianne would know where snakes would be sold to chefs. "Lorianne, you're amazingly helpful. Thanks."

"I already told Detective Carter about it, but he doesn't know that I'm friends with the store owner. Carlton might be chattier with me on the phone with you, and he might remember some things he forgot to tell the detective."

The kitchen door opened and the sous chef called Lorianne's name.

"I've got to go. Come back in an hour, okay?" She hurried back into the kitchen.

"Did you tell Detective Carter about Chris?" Monica asked Shaun.

"I called him as soon as I came back into the restaurant. I knew Chris would take off, but it was more important to make sure you were okay."

His words made her feel both warm and strangely nervous around him. "Thanks."

"I still have to go down to the station to fill out a report," Shaun said. "Why don't you come with me, and then when I'm done, we can come back here?"

"Um…sure." She had been hoping all this time spent in Shaun's company might make her immune to his tall, attractive presence, but it only seemed to be making her more aware of him. She noticed details like the scar above his left eyebrow and the fact that he pulled at the lock of hair at his widow's peak when he was nervous. He also sometimes grimaced and rubbed the left side of his torso when he rose from a chair, and she wondered if he had an old wound there from the border patrol.

No, she wouldn't ask him. The more she knew about him, the more she might feel connected to him. She couldn't fall into that emotional trap, because then she wouldn't be able to climb out. Shaun was too easy to like, too attractive for his own good.

Or for her own good.

At the police station, after Shaun filled out the incident report, Detective Carter sought them out. "Come with me." He led them into a small room at the back of the building that was filled with audio-visual equipment.

"Sit." He gestured to some wheeled chairs in front of a screen, and nodded to a tech seated at another console.

A video came up on the screen in front of them of one of

the streets of downtown Sonoma, but the picture was distorted along the edges, as if the video had been shot with a circular, convex lens.

"This is surveillance from an ATM machine along the same street as Lorianne's Café," Detective Carter said. "The picture is only taken once every six seconds, but we got this photo."

The video, which had been choppy, suddenly froze when it showed a man standing in front of the ATM, obviously performing some bank transaction. But behind him to his right was the figure of a man with a large white florist's box.

"We found out that the box wasn't delivered by a delivery service, but by hand," the detective said. "So we canvassed any surveillance videos around the restaurant to get a photo of the man delivering the box."

The man had his head turned away from the ATM camera. "He was trying to avoid getting his picture taken," Monica said.

The detective nodded. "This is the only picture of him. He avoided any other cameras near the restaurant. He probably parked along one of the side streets and walked to the restaurant, and this was the only surveillance camera he had to avoid."

Monica couldn't quite tell, but he didn't seem very tall or very short. He could be about Phillip Bromley's height, but she wasn't certain. Since the photo was in black and white, she also couldn't be sure of his hair color, but his hair was dark, not light. It was slightly wavy and cut similarly to Phillip's haircut.

"I know it's not a good photo, but do you recognize him?" Detective Carter asked.

"He looks like Phillip Bromley," Shaun said.

"I can't be entirely sure," she said.

"When you were going to meet Mr. Bromley at the restaurant that day, you mentioned that he called you to say he was delayed in traffic, is that correct?"

"Yes. He said there was an overturned truck on 121."

Detective Carter gave a curt nod. "There was an overturned truck that day. It happened at least an hour before you were at the restaurant, and it wasn't moved off the road for two hours."

"So he could have been in traffic."

"He could have heard about it on the radio," Shaun said. "But all the time he could have already been in Sonoma."

Detective Carter nodded. "That's also a possibility."

Monica stared at the photo but just couldn't recognize anything to distinguish who it was. She could have met him anytime in the past few months and wouldn't know him from the averted profile. "I'm sorry, I just can't identify him."

"That's fine," the detective said. "I wanted you to see the picture regardless."

They left the police station and as they were walking back to the café, Monica said, "You really want it to be Phillip Bromley."

Shaun's jaw flexed, but he didn't say anything.

"I'm not saying it isn't Phillip," Monica said gently, "but I also want to point out that if you lose your objectivity in this, it doesn't help us find out who the stalker is."

She wasn't sure how he'd take her words, and was steeling herself for his possible anger, but he chewed on his bottom lip and then glanced at her. "You're right."

His agreement with her made her bold enough to reach out and touch his forearm. His skin was warm under her fingers, and corded with muscle. She also felt a narrow scar that was bumpy under her fingers.

His hand closed over hers, and for a moment, all she could feel was his palm, slightly rough against the back of her hand.

But more than his hand, she felt his strength, his dependability.

Then that same haunting pain returned to his eyes, just a fleeting flash. His hand let go of hers, and she let go of his arm, and the moment was gone.

That pain she'd seen made her want to reach out and soothe him. She wanted to know what had happened to him down at the border to make him quit his job. She wanted to know why his guilt over his sister seemed to cut him so deeply.

No, she shouldn't want him to be vulnerable with her, because then she'd want to be vulnerable with him. Vulnerability would draw them closer, and she needed to keep him at arm's length. She needed to keep her heart at arm's length.

When they returned to the restaurant, there were only a few tables filled, and they looked like patrons only lingering over their coffee after a good meal. The hostesses smiled at Monica and Shaun and one of them led them into the kitchen.

The chefs and other kitchen workers were still busy, but even Monica could tell that the pace wasn't as frantic as the glimpse she'd seen of the kitchen an hour earlier. They passed between long worktables, skirting the stoves and sinks, and the hostess led them into a door at the back of the kitchen.

She knocked, and Lorianne's voice called, "Come on in."

The office was immaculate and organized, but it seemed crowded because of the desk and the file cabinets against the wall. Lorianne sat at her computer, but she waved them into two chairs she'd placed next to her behind the desk. The hostess closed the door behind them.

"Carlton's in San Francisco," Lorianne said. "I already called him to schedule a video chat over the computer with us."

Monica shouldn't have been surprised that Lorianne was so organized. "That's great."

Lorianne set up the internet video camera built into the top of her computer monitor. The angle wasn't wide enough for all three of them, so Shaun scooted to the side so Lorianne and Monica could sit in front of the camera.

With a few clicks of the mouse, Lorianne "called" Carlton with an internet video chat program, and a man's face appeared in the screen. He was bald, but he looked to be only about thirty years old. His dark bushy eyebrows rose above small circular glasses propped on his large Roman nose. "Hi, Lorianne," he said, his voice very deep.

"Hi, Carlton. This is Monica Grant."

"Hi," Monica said.

"The police already called me this morning about that snake," Carlton said. "I can tell you what I told them. I got the order over the internet, and the guy wanted to come in person to pick it up. He even specified a date and time. He paid in cash."

"What did he look like?" Lorianne asked.

Carlton sighed. "You know I'm bad at stuff like that."

"Just try."

He rubbed the top of his head with a large hand. "He was about a foot shorter than me, with lots of brown hair."

"Was it curly like J.W.'s?" Lorianne asked. She seemed to be referring to someone they both knew.

"No, not that curly."

"More like Bobby's?"

"Not that straight. Not that light, either. You know how his hair is always flying around?"

"So not too fine. How about like Bill's hair?"

"Yeah, close to that."

Lorianne picked up her cell phone and scrolled through the photos on it. She showed Monica and Shaun a picture of a man with brown hair, slightly wavy. Much like Phillip's.

"How about his face?" Lorianne asked Carlton. "Round like Chin's?"

"No, more narrow like Boyd's. And his eyes were close together like Boyd's, too."

"See? You're great at this, Carlton." Lorianne again flipped through the pictures on her cell phone and showed them a picture of a man with an oval-shaped face, and eyes a little close together.

Shaun sent Monica a meaningful look, and she knew exactly what he was trying to tell her—*Similar to Phillip's eyes.*

"What was he wearing?" Lorianne asked.

Carlton suddenly perked up. "Do you remember that time I made you watch *Once Upon a Time in the West?*"

Lorianne rolled her eyes. "Yes, but what does that have to do with it?"

"You remember that long coat Charles Bronson and the gunslingers all wore? This guy had a coat just like that, but it was black leather."

Shaun had grown very still and very tense. His hands gripped the arms of the chair so hard that his knuckles stood out against his veins.

"It's called a duster," Shaun said, his voice tight and raw. "It's a leather duster."

"What's wrong?" Lorianne asked him.

Shaun swallowed hard. "When Clare investigated that bottle of snake venom she was sent, the clerk said that the man who bought it wore a black leather duster."

Lorianne's eyes widened. "So it's the same guy."

"More than that," Monica said slowly. "The only man I know who wears a black leather duster just had lunch with me."

When Monica gave a yelp of surprise as she looked inside her post office box, Shaun immediately muscled her aside.

"What's wrong? What is it?" he asked her as he peered inside the box.

"Sorry, I didn't mean to alarm you." Monica pointed to a large manila envelope in the box. "That's the clinic's business proposal. I've been waiting for it to arrive."

Shaun felt silly for shoving her aside as if there had been a bomb in the post office box. Well, better safe than sorry. He cleared his throat as he stepped aside and let her retrieve her mail. "Any notes from the stalker?"

She flipped through the envelopes. "No." She sighed in relief, then frowned. "I hate how just the simple act of getting my mail is stressful."

"We'll find him. He'll come after you, and when he does, I'll be there to protect you and get him."

Her look was trusting. "I know you will."

He felt an uncomfortable twisting in his gut. He exhaled forcefully and glanced around before ushering her out of the post office. "I wish you'd let me drive," he said as she pulled her car keys out of her slacks pocket.

"I wish you'd stop nagging me about it," she retorted, but with a teasing glint in her eye. "It's my car."

"If something happens, I'm better at defensive driving tactics than you are."

"I disagree." She unlocked the car doors. "I'm more familiar with this car and better able to control it than you are. Besides which, I've driven this car all through the streets of San Francisco and Oakland, in both good and bad neighborhoods. I know how to drive defensively."

Privately, Shaun doubted she'd know how to avoid a PIT maneuver—a way of ramming her car at an angle that would make it spin out. At the very least he could keep an eye out to see if any cars looked suspicious and to maybe get a glimpse of the driver, which he couldn't have done if he were driving.

"You said that your friend lives on J Street?" Monica

steered her car out of the post office parking lot and took a right, heading away from the center of downtown Sonoma.

"He has a house on the outskirts of downtown."

"A house? That's prime real estate."

"Nathan's family has lived in Sonoma for a few generations, but I didn't meet him until I moved down south."

"You worked with him on the border patrol?"

"No, he worked for the Los Angeles Police Department. We met during a joint investigation several years ago, and I found out he used to live in Sonoma. And now he's back here again."

"He's working for the Sonoma PD?"

"No, he was injured in a gunfight with an L.A. drug gang—a bullet shattered a bone in his leg—so he's retired from police work."

Monica kept her attention on the road, but her eyes softened with sympathy. "That must be hard on him."

Shaun didn't know how to respond to that. He'd visited Nathan Fischer about three years ago. Shaun had been up in northern California for Christmas, and he'd stopped by to see Nathan, who had retired only a few months earlier. The strong, tall man he remembered had seemed wounded, broken, but not in body so much as in some deep inner place. He hadn't seen him since, but when Shaun had called to ask if they could come over today, Nathan's voice had seemed more cheerful than three years ago.

Nathan's family's three-story house was on a quiet street off the main roads of downtown Sonoma, with a small front yard bordered by a picket fence. Unlike the other houses on the street, which boasted modern stucco walls and new roofing, Nathan's house hadn't been renovated anytime in the past forty years. However, it showed signs of meticulous upkeep.

They parked along the street and entered the little gate, picking their way up the flagstone walkway to the front porch. Someone had planted peonies along the sides of the walkway, which were blooming in the warm California spring air.

Nathan opened the front door and pushed open the outer screen door before they'd even climbed the front steps. "Good to see you, Shaun."

Here was the Nathan he remembered from the LAPD, tall and confident. His straight brown hair was a little longer than it had been before, making him look younger. But even though he smiled at Shaun, there was something about his eyes that seemed empty.

Shaun shook his hand. "Nathan, this is Monica Grant."

She smiled and shook his hand. "Thank you for seeing us today."

"I always have time for friends. Come on in." Nathan limped as he led them into the front living room, but at least he wasn't in a wheelchair anymore. "Sorry about the mess. Mom had some visitors today." He cleared away a few used coffee cups from the oak coffee table. "Coffee? I just made a fresh pot."

"Please." Monica sank into an overstuffed chair. Shaun dropped into the couch next to her.

Nathan brought out three steaming mugs and placed them on the coffee table, then eased himself into the recliner, wincing a little.

"Leg still bothering you?" Shaun asked.

"Only today," Nathan said. "I did work on the house all day yesterday before going to work last night. I just overdid it."

"What do you do?" Monica asked.

"I'm in charge of security night shift at Glencove Towers."

Shaun raised his eyebrows. "Nice gig." The Glencove building in Sonoma was full of very high-end condos.

"I was lucky to get the job, with my bum leg." He had said

it without hesitation, but he blinked away a flash of pain. He sipped his coffee. "What did you need to talk to me about?"

"You still have contacts down in LAPD?"

"Sure."

"Can you ask them to look into something for me? A cold case."

Nathan's eyes narrowed as they regarded Shaun. "Is this about your sister again?"

"I have more information this time—"

"Do you suddenly have proof against Phillip Bromley?" Nathan demanded.

Shaun pressed his lips together and shook his head.

"I told you this before, Shaun. Without proof, the police can't go digging around the son of a bank CEO. I even showed you evidence I shouldn't have because you asked me to." Nathan sighed.

"I'm not asking you to get the LAPD to investigate Phillip Bromley." He could do that himself, on his own. "But Monica received a note from a stalker that quoted the same line from the poet Byron that my sister received."

Nathan's gaze sharpened. "Before, when you asked me to look up Byron's poetry in other stalking cases, I came up with nothing."

"I don't know why, maybe he messed up this time, but he used the same phrase. Maybe because he was sending Monica a dead snake with the note. He threatened to hurt her if she didn't stop work on her free children's clinic—another free clinic, Nathan. Clare was working on a free family planning clinic. You can't tell me that's all just coincidence."

He didn't answer at first, then said, "No, I can't."

"We talked to the man in San Francisco who sold the snake, and he described the man as looking like Phillip Bromley, including wearing his black leather duster."

"A duster? Like the guy who bought the snake venom that he sent to Clare," Nathan said.

Shaun nodded. "Sonoma PD got an ATM picture of the guy who delivered the dead snake and the note."

"We can't tell it's Phillip," Monica said, "but the man is about the same height, build and coloring. And when you take into account the black leather duster, it makes for even more coincidences."

Nathan leaned back in the recliner and stared unseeing at the far wall as he thought. "I doubt they'd reopen the investigation."

"I'm not asking them to," Shaun said. "But maybe they can look into the evidence from that night again with fresh eyes."

"They may not be able to find new evidence to prove the stalker killed Clare," Monica said, "but anything they find could help the Sonoma PD catch the man stalking me, especially now when it seems obvious it's the same man."

Nathan nodded slowly. "I'll talk to some guys I know in L.A. At the very least, I can have the files from Clare's death sent to Sonoma PD to look at."

The mention of his sister's death made Shaun's jaw clench. Would he ever reach a point when the thought of her didn't prick him with so much pain and guilt?

"Thanks," Shaun said.

"I'm not promising anything," Nathan warned.

"We know," Monica said.

Nathan nodded to her. "I'm sorry this is happening to you. I'm sorry it happened to Clare."

They rose to go, but Monica said to Nathan, "You don't have to walk us out. It's not as if the front door is hard to find." She smiled as she said it.

Nathan had started to rise from the recliner, but stopped when Monica spoke. Some of that strange empty look left his eyes as he looked at her, and Shaun realized why he was so attracted to her.

Monica had a gift for healing.

Not just as a nurse, but also touching that dark space inside and making the pain lessen a little. That was why Nathan responded to her expression and her words.

That was why Shaun had been so drawn to her from the moment he saw her again in Sonoma. Aside from their physical attraction, the dark place inside him was drawn to her lightness, that ability she had of helping him feel lighter.

Except his darkness was just too dark for anyone to see, least of all Monica Grant. He'd rather hold on to it and keep it in check himself.

Shaun shook Nathan's hand again, and they left the house. As they approached where they'd parked the car, the scent of some weird cigarette smoke made his nose burn.

Then he realized that the hood of her car wasn't entirely closed.

Shaun shoved Monica behind him and scanned the empty street. There were silent houses all around, some with sheer drapes over the large front windows that could be hiding a watcher in the shadows. He would be observing them, maybe with binoculars, enjoying Shaun's futile alarm, Monica's shock and fear.

The thought made him grind his teeth in frustration.

"Shaun." Monica clutched at his arm, her fingers digging into his skin. "The backseat."

He took a few steps forward.

White paper had been savagely shredded all over her backseat. Her clinic's business proposal. Even the manila envelope had been ripped into tiny pieces, as if the stalker could destroy her plans for the free clinic if he destroyed this paper evidence.

"Don't show fear," Shaun told her. "He wants you to be afraid."

"I'm not afraid." Her voice shook.

He searched the street again. Had that curtain moved? Had sunlight glinted off something in another window? He couldn't tell where the stalker might be hiding. If he could disable her car alarm, he definitely could break into some of these houses, some of which didn't have house alarms.

"We can't just stand here," Monica said. "We have to call the police."

Shaun didn't want to. He wanted to wait to see if the stalker showed himself. But as the minutes ticked by, he realized it was useless. The stalker could have exited any house's back door and escaped over a back fence, and they'd never see him.

"Fine. But let's do this inside Nathan's house."

They hurried back and surprised Nathan, whose hands were sudsy with dishwashing soap. "What happened?"

"The stalker broke into Monica's car," Shaun said. "We need to call the police."

Nathan's spine stiffened and he quickly pulled them inside. He looked up and down the block before closing the front door. "Did you see him?"

"No, but I think he was watching us from one of the other houses."

Monica inhaled sharply, but she didn't say anything. Instead, she pulled out her cell phone and dialed. "Aunt Becca? I need you to call Detective Carter for me. I'm at 451 J Street. The stalker broke into my car." Her voice wobbled and her face had gone pale, but she kept her shoulders straight and continued, "I'm fine, I promise. Aunt Becca, did you already deliver to the dry cleaner those coats we gave you?"

Shaun and Nathan exchanged confused looks.

"This morning? Call them right away and ask them not to clean them. It's important." She hung up.

"Your coats?" Shaun was starting to understand Monica enough by now to know that she wouldn't ask about something frivolous unless she had a good reason.

She nodded. "If I can get to those coats before they're dry cleaned, I might have a clue about the stalker." Her face was still tense, but she had a triumphant gleam in her eye. "He might have made his first mistake."

SIX

Monica had to wait almost two and a half days before she could see if she was right, and it seemed like an eternity. When Aunt Becca called the dry cleaner to stop the cleaning order, she'd just caught them before they closed for the weekend.

So Monica spent Saturday helping out at the spa since her dad was talking with Shaun's father about his hotel plans and Naomi was taking time off to work on her wedding plans. Monica gave Shaun the weekend off since she'd be surrounded by family and also Detective Carter, who joined Aunt Becca for church on Sunday.

There were no notes, no gruesome gifts. But the reprieve only put Monica on edge, waiting for the other shoe to drop.

Monday morning, she waited in the foyer of the house for Aunt Becca to get ready to go and for Shaun to arrive to pick them up. They were going to the dry cleaner to be there the minute they opened that morning.

A knock sounded at the door. "I'll get it, Evita," Monica called to the housekeeper. She checked the video monitor that showed the front stoop and saw their regular postman, Mas, so she disabled the house alarm and unlocked the front door.

He smiled as he saw her. "Good morning, Miss Monica."

He passed over a bundle of mail—just envelopes, no packages or florist boxes.

Monica didn't realize she'd been tense until her muscles relaxed. She took the envelopes from the postman.

"Have a good day," he said.

"Thanks, Mas." She closed the door and reengaged the alarm. It hadn't been such a habit a year ago, but when an intruder broke into Rachel's room, they all had decided it was better to be safe than sorry. Now, she was doubly glad she reengaged the alarm almost without thinking these days.

She flipped through the mail. Bill, bill, advertisement. A personal note to her father—she set that on the hallway table. Some legal-sized business envelopes for her father also found their way onto the table.

Then she saw a manilla envelope addressed to her.

The ground tilted under her feet for a sickening moment, and she reached out to grab the edge of the table. Her heart knocked against her chest. *Calm down. It's just an envelope.*

But there was a faint scent of cigarette smoke, the same smell from her car.

They had to get to those coats so she could find out if she was right about that cigarette smell.

The envelope trembled in her hand, so she set it down. Gloves. She'd get gloves. Not just to help Detective Carter collect evidence, but also because she couldn't bear the thought of touching something the stalker also touched.

She had plenty of exam gloves next to the first-aid kit in the library. She grabbed the entire box and also removed a scalpel handle and fresh blade that she kept in the kit.

She almost cut open her finger as she attached the blade to the scalpel because her hands were shaking, but she grit her teeth and focused, and the blade went on smoothly. She sliced open the top of the envelope, not touching the gummed section of the flap, and upended the contents onto the table.

Photos of her, candids taken with a zoom lens. Some with Shaun, some without. A few from early Sunday morning, but none from that afternoon or evening when she'd gone to lunch with her family and then gone shopping in Napa. The pictures looked like they'd been processed at any automated photo service.

She forced herself to look through the photos one by one. Several had bull's eyes drawn over her face with a red marker pen, and the sight made her shudder.

The strong smell of that distinctive type of cigarette wafted up from the pictures. He'd handled the photos a bit before putting them in the envelope, enough so that the cigarette he'd been smoking, or maybe just the scent on his clothes, had attached to the surface of the pictures.

She picked up the envelope and shook it upside down to see if there were any other photos, and a white square piece of paper fell out.

I could have killed you at any time, but I am merciful. Stop work on your clinic now before you get hurt. I don't want to kill you, but I will if you persist.

As she picked the note up between her gloved fingers, she realized it was very thick, creamy white stock paper. She held it up to the light streaming in through the windows above, and saw a tiny Japanese maple leaf-shaped watermark on the bottom right corner.

She knew this paper. It was a distinctive watermark used by one of her favorite stationery shops in San Francisco, a very expensive store situated on Union Square. She didn't buy much from them because she couldn't justify paying so much for just paper, but she had purchased some pretty stationery for her sisters for Christmas a few months ago, and she had also bought some paper for business correspondence, all of which had this watermark.

Again, a high-end store, like the place he'd bought the snakes.

"Okay, I'm ready…" Aunt Becca paused as she reached the bottom steps of the stairs. "Monica, what's wrong?"

Monica didn't answer fast enough, and her aunt's eye fell on the envelope and pictures on the table, and the note still in her hand.

"Give that to me," Aunt Becca said firmly.

"No—"

"I raised you from the time you were eight years old," her aunt said in a hard voice Monica hadn't ever heard from her before. "You girls are like my daughters, and you will not lie to me and tell me that's not what I think it is." She reached over to the table and grabbed an extra glove, snapping it on. "Hand it over."

She did.

Aunt Becca's delicate skin seemed to grow more papery as she read the note. She whipped out her cell phone. "I'm calling Horatio right now."

"Do it later. I want to get to the dry cleaner." Until the words flew out of her mouth, Monica hadn't realized she could sound so normal even with the storm raging inside her stomach.

"The dry cleaner can wait."

"What's going on?" Her father wheeled himself into the front foyer. She knew he'd been in the kitchen and had hoped he couldn't hear her talking to her aunt, but apparently he had.

Aunt Becca hesitated, but then held out the notecard. "Don't touch it without gloves," she warned him. At that moment, Detective Carter answered the phone and she said, "Hello, Horatio? You need to come to the house right now."

Monica's father pulled a handkerchief from his pocket and took the card between the cloth folds. His bushy eyebrows, once golden but now ash-blond, settled low over his thunderous eyes as he read the note.

The churning storm in Monica's stomach turned into a tornado as he glared at her.

"You are going to stop this clinic nonsense right now," he said.

His commanding voice did what it always did to her— made her set her chin and fire back, "No, I'm not."

"Don't be a stubborn fool."

"I'm trying not to be a victim."

"What good is your pride when your family is hurt?" her father raged. "This man knows our home address."

"He could have found it out anytime in the past few weeks," Monica answered. "All he had to do was follow one of us home from the spa."

Her father didn't reply, but his lips were bloodless and his eyes sparked.

Aunt Becca got off the phone. "Horatio's on his way, and I asked him to pick up the coats from the dry cleaner, too."

"You did?" Monica felt faintly embarrassed to have her aunt's boyfriend picking up their laundry, but then realized it might be a good thing after all.

The home telephone rang, and Evita's voice floated faintly from the kitchen as she answered. In a minute, she'd entered the front foyer. "Mr. Grant, Mr. O'Neill is on the phone for you."

Her father wheeled himself toward the library, but he said over his shoulder, "I am going to talk to you about this later." The library door shut behind him.

Monica closed her eyes. "All he does is talk *to* me," she said softly.

Aunt Becca's arm wrapped around her shoulders. "He's only concerned for you."

"One of these days I'd like him to actually listen to me." She could have explained why the clinic was so important to her. She could have explained the precautions she'd been taking to protect herself, and how they'd been drawing the stalker out little by little. There was so much they were discovering about him. They were getting closer to catching him, she could feel it.

At that moment, the doorbell rang. "That'll be Shaun."

It was. He looked through the photos and his expression grew darker. Then he said, "Do you have a camera? Detective Carter will take these with him, so let's take pictures so we have a copy."

"Good idea." She went up to her room and returned with her laptop and a digital camera, and they took pictures of the pictures. Monica set her laptop up on the dining room table and they had just connected the camera for uploading the pictures when the doorbell rang again.

They let in Detective Carter with his arms full of dry cleaning. Once they were all inside and settled into the living room, Monica handed the envelope to the detective. "We used gloves when handling it." She handed him a pair.

"Good." He pulled the gloves on and looked through the pictures.

When he came to the note, Monica said, "Hold it up to the light." When he did, she continued, "That's a very distinctive watermark used by Greywell's Stationers, a store at Union Square in San Francisco."

"How do you know?"

"I bought stationery there for my sisters for Christmas a few months ago. I also bought some paper for business correspondence."

"All this stationer's paper has this watermark?"

"Yes, it's a Japanese maple leaf. Greywell's is a very high-end store. I don't usually buy much from them."

"Their paper and journals are very popular with many of the wealthier spa clients," Aunt Becca said.

Shaun said, "More evidence that he's wealthy."

She nodded. "At first I thought he might just be willing to pay a lot to scare me. Clare's snake venom wouldn't come cheap, and neither did the dead snakes. And maybe that tourist guy would only pose as a decoy if he paid him five thousand dollars. But stationery like this is a luxury for people who have a lot of money."

Detective Carter nodded, then put the envelope and pictures in an evidence bag. "Now, why did you need me to pick up these coats?" He reached to where he'd dropped the coats on the sofa and handed them to Monica.

She pawed through them, pulling out three of them. "These are coats I wore to three events in the past two weeks. Did you notice the cigarette smell on the photos?"

"The same as your car."

"And the same as the snake in the florist's box. When I first got the snake, I knew there was something familiar about the smoke smell. It's not from a normal cigarette. It's something European, maybe. But I couldn't remember where I'd smelled it before, until I smelled it at the car."

She sniffed the first coat, but it only had a very slight cigarette smell, maybe from transfer from another coat. Same with the second coat. But the third coat, the one she'd worn to the Zoe banquet, had the strong odor clinging to the shoulders and sleeves.

"Here, smell this." She passed it to the detective. "I remembered smelling that cigarette scent when I walked into a coatroom to get my coat at the end of some event, but I couldn't remember which one. That's why I needed the coats before they'd been dry cleaned. I wore that one to the Zoe banquet."

Shaun's eyes were like gas burners. "That means you met him there."

"Yes, a little over a week ago." Monica gave the detective the information about the banquet.

"I'll talk to the event director and get a guest list," Carter said. "Do you remember who you talked to that night about your clinic?"

"It was about twenty people, but some of them were women. I got people's business cards, but I have to figure out which card I got at which event. I'll get the list to you."

"Do it quickly." He gave her a hard look with his steel gray eyes. "Don't think for a moment that I don't know what you're doing."

She returned his gaze. "One of them might be the stalker, but the rest of them are still investors for my free clinic, Detective. I'm not about to completely ignore them until you catch this guy."

Aunt Becca gave a small moan. "I'm so glad your father is still talking with Mr. O'Neill and didn't hear you say that."

"She's hired me to protect her," Shaun said. "I'll make sure nothing happens to her."

Aunt Becca smiled warmly at him. "I'm so glad she has you, Shaun. You make me feel so much better about all this."

But then she surprised Monica by turning to her and saying, "I don't know why this clinic is so important to you, but I know you have your reasons. And I know you hate how this stalker is trying to manipulate you, and I can understand your anger. Just don't be too reckless, okay?"

Her aunt's words were like a mug of hot cocoa. Aunt Becca had always seemed to understand her so much better than her father, than her sisters. Maybe because at heart, Aunt Becca was a bit of a wild child like Monica.

The detective finally rose to leave, and Aunt Becca walked him out to his car.

Shaun and Monica headed back to the dining room, where the camera had uploaded the photos. They looked through them one by one on her computer.

She smiled as she saw the photo of the notecard.

Shaun's eyes narrowed. "What are you planning?"

"Those investors from the Zoe banquet? I'm going to invite them to my party."

"Do you really think that's wise?"

"Every time I deliberately ignore his warnings, he does something to reveal more about himself."

Shaun looked thoughtful. "Mostly true," he conceded.

"He must be stewing with anger to be doing this against me."

"Or crazy."

"Or both. If I get him upset, he might reveal more than he intended to."

"Or he might come after you. He'll skip the threatening part and head right into the murdering part."

She turned to face him. "But you'll protect me, right?" Without thinking, she touched his hand, and then realized what a mistake it was.

His skin was warmer than she expected it to be, the tendons tight under her touch. He seemed startled at her touch for a brief moment, then his hand turned over and he enfolded her fingers in his.

"Yes, I'll do everything I can to protect you."

"I'm counting on you." She yanked her hand away harder than she intended to. She cleared her throat and looked at the notecard again. "I need you to be on your game."

"More than usual?" he asked dryly.

She gave him a sidelong look. "More than usual. Because

I'm going to send the invitations on the same Greywell's stationery that the stalker used."

Would he notice? She hoped so. She was throwing down the gauntlet.

Shaun squinted at the copy of the stalker photo in his hand, then at the church across the street. He took a step to his right, then a step to his left.

"Well?" Monica called to him. She stood on the church front steps, in the same position as in the photo.

Except Shaun couldn't figure out the angle of where the stalker had been when he took the shot.

Maybe it was the fact the photo had been taken with a zoom lens. He pulled out a camera with a zoom lens that he'd borrowed from his brother Brady and spied Monica through the lens. It wasn't quite right....

Then he remembered to squat down, since the stalker was a few inches shorter than he was. Except the picture still didn't match what he saw in his camera. He kept getting lower and lower until he was almost on his knees. That's when he realized the stalker must have been sitting. Yes, that was the angle. He gave Monica a thumb's-up and she hurried across the street to him, checking for traffic before she crossed the road.

He spun around to see what was directly behind him. He stood in front of the window of Captain Caffeine's Espresso, a new coffeeshop. The storefront had been a rundown donut shop until the owner, Thomas Chadwick, had bought it and renovated it. Now it looked like it belonged on the streets of Rome. Tables and chairs were set up throughout the wide space, and there was one directly behind the window where Shaun was standing, in the corner of the shop, against the wall.

However, because it had become so popular with both

locals and tourists, the café was typically full of people, like it was today. Would anyone have noted a man who sat at the table in the corner?

Thomas Chadwick, Captain Caffeine himself, was behind the counter making the coffee drinks at the huge gleaming espresso machine. He smiled and nodded to Monica when he saw her. "Want your usual? I've got a white chocolate mocha with your name on it."

"That would be great, Tom. But I also wanted to know if you could help me out."

"Sure."

"Did you or any of your staff notice a guy sitting at that corner table Sunday morning, around nine o'clock?" That's when they'd figured out the photo had been taken. They'd had to figure out the times for each of the photos she received.

Tom sent a squinty glance at the table, then frowned as he frothed milk in a frothing pitcher. "That table at nine? I should remember, we don't have many people that early on Sunday morning. Why?"

"Well...I think he was spying on me coming out of church." Monica's light tone didn't make too much out of it.

Tom's mouth quirked up at the corners as he tapped the bottom of the frothing pitcher against the smooth counter. "Secret admirer?"

"More like annoying admirer," Monica said.

"Let's see...Sunday morning I was working the machine most of the time because my other barista is on baby leave. But I did walk around to straighten tables around eight-thirty or so."

He paused as he poured the frothed milk into a wide-mouthed latte mug, creating a fern leaf design in the top. He handed it to a waiting customer, then turned back to Monica. "I think I do remember a guy there. Does your admirer smoke?"

Shaun's shoulders tensed. After Monica had sent the party invitations, she and Shaun had spent the past few days tracking down the camera angles for each of the photos and interviewing people. The eyewitness accounts had been pretty varied—some said the man was blond, others brown, others redheaded. This was the first time someone had mentioned the cigarette smoke.

Monica quickly replied, "Yes."

"Yeah, I could smell it on the jacket he was wearing. Not your usual cigarette smell, but something more harsh."

"What kind of jacket was he wearing?" Shaun asked.

Tom gestured to the top of his thigh. "Regular sports jacket. Dark brown. At first I thought he might be going to church, but he had on jeans and heavy workboots. I remember that because he tracked a bit of mud into the store."

"I saw him, too," said the girl manning the register, who had been listening. "There weren't many people, so when we weren't taking orders, I was chatting with Angie behind the counter, and I remember seeing him at the table."

"What else did he look like?" Shaun asked.

Tom shrugged. "He was just a normal-looking guy. Brown hair. I think brown eyes. Marla, help me out here. Did you pay more attention to what he looked like?"

"Big nose," Marla said.

It sounded like Phillip, especially the big nose. "Were his eyes close together?" Shaun asked.

Marla shook his head. "No, I don't think so."

So it hadn't been Phillip? But what about the cigarette smoke? Or perhaps it was just part of how eyewitnesses weren't always accurate? He remembered the blond/brown/redheaded men people had claimed to see.

"I think he was tanned," Marla said.

"He was?" Tom said. "I didn't think so. The entire store is dark in the mornings because the window faces west."

Marla shrugged. "I thought he was, but I could be wrong. If he was tanned, it wasn't more than a lot of the other tourists."

Tanned? Phillip was rather pale. But even Marla wasn't certain about that.

"Yeah, that's all I can think of," the girl said before another customer came up to order.

Tom made Monica's white chocolate mocha, which Shaun had to admit smelled fantastic. Then Tom poured a cup of brewed coffee and handed it to Shaun.

He dug in his back pocket for his wallet, but Tom waved him away. "On the house. Just make sure you protect this girl against those annoying admirers." He winked at the two of them, then set to work to make the next customer's drink.

As they exited the espresso shop, the back of Shaun's neck buzzed angrily. He scanned the street even as he grabbed Monica's arm to pull her closer to him. He felt her muscles tense.

"Is he watching us?" she whispered.

"He might be. He's probably laughing at us, enjoying seeing us try to track him down."

She shivered. "I don't feel like he's laughing. I feel like he's angry."

Her words made him realize that he felt that, too. The prickling feeling of being watched was nothing like when he'd known the stalker was observing them at Monica's car several days ago. Then, he had almost felt the stalker's glee at upsetting them.

Now, the feeling of being watched was like a burning gaze, ugly and snarling. What had changed? Were they getting too close?

"Let's get to the car." He moved her swiftly across the street to where they'd parked the car in the empty church parking lot. Monica had gotten in and started the engine even before he'd climbed into the passenger seat and closed the door. She pulled out of the parking lot at a fast clip.

But as she drove, he noticed her hands shaking where they gripped the steering wheel. She gave a sobbing breath. "I'm tired of this. I'm so tired of being watched."

"Pull over."

"No." She inhaled long and deep, then let it out. "I'm fine. It just got to me for a moment."

He knew she wasn't fine, but he also didn't know what to say to her. He himself kept his feelings under control like a closed soda bottle that had been shaken up. Feelings were messy. It was easier to just do his work, keep himself busy, and eventually it would be okay.

Was he talking about Monica or himself?

She drove back to her home, but after parking the car in the multi-car garage, she rested her forehead against the steering wheel and closed her eyes.

"You're okay," he said to her.

"I will be," she whispered. "I just need a moment. I can't let Dad see me like this."

"You mean, upset?"

"He would say, 'I told you so.' It's his favorite thing to say to me. Maybe because I almost never do what he wants me to do."

"Never?" Shaun had always been the straight-arrow son, the one who always listened to his dad. Maybe because he was the oldest, and it had been his job to watch out for his siblings when his dad was gone working on another hotel.

"Dad always wants me to do things that just aren't me. I went into nursing rather than working at the spa. I took a job at a hospital in San Francisco rather than a posh position Dad had gotten for me at a private health resort in Sonoma. I'm working on this free children's clinic rather than becoming a resident nurse at the spa."

"Maybe he just wants you close to him."

She shook her head. "Dad has always wanted to rein me in. His wild child."

Yes, he could see how Monica would be the wild one. Full of energy and fire. Augustus Grant seemed to be intense in his focus, but not as passionate as his youngest daughter.

"Do you know what's the dumbest part of it all? I'm always so surprised when Dad just dismisses anything I do as unimportant. Most of the time, what I do is something he didn't approve of anyway, so why do I feel so hurt when he doesn't value any of my accomplishments?"

He didn't have an answer for her. His father had always made him feel that his decisions were his own, and had supported him no matter what he chose.

But Shaun did know one thing—the hurt in Monica's voice was real, and everything inside him wanted to protect her from the things that wounded her, be her human shield.

He didn't understand her relationship with her father, but he'd do what he could to protect her.

She took another deep breath, and her porcelain face smoothed. He couldn't help being amazed at how beautiful she was.

They entered the house through the door from the garage. "Let's put Tom's description of the man up on the board," Monica said. They'd created a master board on the wall of her bedroom, which was so large it had a small sitting area on one side. They'd been putting self-adhesive notes on one wall with all the information they'd collected about the stalker.

As they headed up the stairs, Evita came out from the kitchen. "Monica, there's a call for you on the house phone."

Shaun didn't think anything of it, but Monica suddenly tensed. "From whom?" she asked.

"He said something about a bank, but he was speaking so quickly I wasn't sure."

"Probably a telemarketer," Shaun said.

But Monica's teeth worried her bottom lip for a moment. Finally she said, "I'll take the call in the library."

She walked stiffly into the library and zeroed in on the large desk on the far side, in front of the window. But instead of picking up the receiver, she punched the speakerphone button. "Hello?" she said.

A rasping breath sounded, and the skin on his arms crawled.

Then a low voice uttered, "Monica."

It was the same voice as the stalker, Shaun realized.

SEVEN

The voice cut through her like wind in the dead of January. Monica began to shiver.

"Monica," he said again, and she realized his voice shook. "How dare you?" His voice was low and disguised, but his anger sounded through the room louder than a shout.

Shaun fumbled for his cell phone, scrolling through a few screens, and then he set it down next to the phone. Monica looked closer and saw he had activated a voice recording application.

"How dare you call me?" She tried to sound braver than she felt.

"I told you to stop work on this clinic," he said, his words clipped. "You haven't listened to me."

"Yes, I have." She wanted to see how he would respond.

"Liar!" he shouted.

He knew about Monica's party. The invitations had clearly stated it was for her free children's clinic project.

Which meant he had been one of the forty people invited.

Somehow, this knowledge only made her more afraid.

The voice then spat insults at her, using language foul enough to make her cringe. She felt as if she were shriveling.

But then a warm strong arm wrapped around her shoulders and held her close. Shaun's musky scent covered her senses, leather with a hint of pine that blanketed her. The man flung arrows at her, but Shaun was her shield.

"You cancel this party," the man said, "or I *will* hurt you." He hung up.

In the silence that followed, Shaun's arm tightened around her.

"Was that him?" Her father's outraged voice shot out from the doorway.

He wheeled himself into the room, his expression livid. "He called the house? He knows our number?"

Shaun turned off the voice recorder app on his phone and stowed it into his pocket. Monica watched him, rather than answering her father. She didn't know what to say. The voice had struck at her, and she felt vulnerable.

"You'll stop work on this clinic right now," her father roared. "It was a stupid idea from the beginning. I told you that, but you're too pigheaded to see when something is doomed to fail."

Her father's words were almost as horrible as the stalker's. She felt herself shriveling again. He was being completely unreasonable, but she didn't have the strength to fight him right now.

"Mr. Grant," Shaun said, his voice steely. "You need to *back off.*"

No one had ever stood up to her father for her before. Her sisters tried, but she never let them fight her battles for her. She'd never before felt so vulnerable that she couldn't hold her own against him.

But now, in this moment when she'd been weak, Shaun was strong. For her.

At first, her father looked as astonished as Monica felt. Then he snapped, "You're out of line." Her father's temper had always been a match for her own, although he hid it better from other people. In a sense, he and Monica were too much alike. But Monica freely exercised her emotions and instincts in order to help people while her father channeled his emotions into his vision for his spa.

"No, I think you're out of line," Shaun replied. "I realize you're worried about Monica's safety, but what you're saying isn't true."

Worried? He hadn't sounded worried. He'd sounded disdainful.

"I know what's true and what's not," he shot back. "She's my daughter."

"You're seeing her as your daughter, not as a businesswoman, and she's both."

"She's not. She thinks she's a businesswoman, but she hasn't proven it to me." His mouth formed a slash across his tight face.

It was like it always was. He would never acknowledge anything she chose to do if it wasn't in line with his plans for her.

Well, she wasn't going to give in—not to the stalker, and not to her father's disapproval of her.

Monica reached out and touched Shaun's arm. He looked at her, then took a step away from her father.

"We're done, Dad." She turned and walked out of the library.

"You come back here," he said.

"You've said everything you need to say," Shaun told him, then hurried after her. He closed the library door after him.

She stumbled through the house, feeling like a blind woman, but finally she found a back door and tripped out into the rose garden.

There weren't many roses, only a few early ones that had just opened their buds. But the bright spots of color lining the walkway relaxed her. She didn't remember much about her mother because she'd been only a child when her mother had been killed by a drunk driver, but Monica did have a hazy memory of walking through the rosebushes, holding her mom's hand.

She reached the center of the garden before she realized Shaun was only a few steps behind her, watching out for her. She turned into his arms and began to cry.

Not delicate, beautiful tears, but heaving sobs tore out of her. She clung to Shaun, holding him tight, because he was a rock in the storm of her fear and pain.

When she finally quieted, she stood there, her face pressed to his tear-soaked cotton shirt. "I'm sorry about your shirt," she mumbled.

"I needed to wash it, anyway," he quipped. "I try to do it once a year."

She laughed at his dumb joke, and for a moment, she thought she'd start crying again. But she took a deep breath and felt his strength seep into her.

His hands reached up to cup her face, his thumbs wiping away her tears. She saw his face dimly through her swollen eyes, but then his head blocked out the sun, and he bent down to kiss her.

His kiss was tentative at first, as if he wanted to give her something precious but wasn't sure how to do it. But when she leaned into him, he deepened the kiss. His fingers caressed her skin in a comforting touch, soothing away the harshness of her argument with her father, of the stalker's ugly phone call.

He was someone she could so easily depend on.

The thought made her gently pull away. She didn't want to depend on him, she didn't want to get involved with someone like him. Ultimately, it would only cause her worry and pain. She forced herself to remember why she'd quit the Emergency Room, of the heartbreaking times she'd witnessed the pain of women who had lost their brave husbands. She had vowed she'd never be one of them.

Shaun could never be anything other than who he was, a protector. She wouldn't want him to change. But it also meant he could never be hers. She wouldn't let that happen.

She wiped her eyes, wishing for a handkerchief and settling for the cuffs of her shirt. She turned away from him and continued walking slowly through the rose garden.

He fell into step beside her. Neither of them spoke, maybe because they didn't want to have to acknowledge what had just happened.

"It's not too late to stop work on this clinic," he said. "There's nothing wrong with being afraid."

"I'm not afraid." She wasn't as long as he was with her. "Everything the stalker does brings us a step closer to him."

"I don't see how a threatening phone call brought us any closer."

"It was the number he dialed," she said.

"What do you mean?"

"When Evita told me someone had called the home telephone number and asked for me, I knew something was wrong. The home phone number is unlisted, and I never give it out to anyone—not to banks, not to my credit card company, not even for my library card. I always use either my cell phone number or the number of my apartment in San Francisco."

"That's why you immediately put the call on speakerphone," he said.

"I wasn't sure if it would be the stalker, but I knew there could be something important. So now the question is—How did he discover my home phone number?"

They needed this next clue to be one more step closer to finding the stalker, but it was like trying to dig a needle out of a haystack.

Shaun rubbed his tired eyes. After looking through Monica's credit card statements and bills and other paper files for the past couple hours, the numbers and letters were starting to swim in his vision. They'd checked everything—frequent flyer memberships, rental cars, library card, grocery store mailing lists and dozens of online retailers, anything that would have required information for an account. Anyone devious enough could call up a store or business and get a clerk or customer service rep to recite the phone number listed on Monica's account.

She sat back in her chair and sighed. "Nothing?"

"Nothing," he said. They'd called all the places she'd done business, according to all her records, but they all had either her cell phone number or her San Francisco apartment number in their records, not the home telephone number.

She flung her hands up. "How in the world did he get my home phone number?"

Something about her phrasing made him pause. "We're looking at this the wrong way."

"What do you mean?"

"You said, your home phone number. But you're not the only one who lives here."

She straightened in her chair. "Of course! My sisters or father or aunt could have given out this number to some business, and the stalker could have found a way to get that business to give him the phone number."

"Can you get to your family's papers?"

"Dad's might be hard, but definitely my sisters' and my aunt's personal papers. I'll call them first to ask." She took out her cell phone.

An hour later, he was sifting through Becca's credit card statement from a few months ago and saw a charge for International Theater. "What's this?" He showed it to Monica.

She frowned at it for a moment, then snapped her fingers.

"It's a video rental place downtown. They specialize in international movies. Aunt Becca likes to rent Korean soap operas on DVD."

"Do you need to be a member to rent DVDs?"

"I'm not sure."

"Let's find out." He pulled out the Yellow Pages book, found the DVD rental place, and called them using the phone on Monica's desk, putting it on speakerphone.

"Hi, Ms. Itoh," said a young woman when she answered the phone. "What can I help you with today?"

Monica's expression was bewildered.

Shaun gestured for her to respond. He had a feeling he knew what had happened.

"Hi, there. Uh…how'd you know it was me?" Monica said.

"Oh, well, the other day, after your brother-in-law came by to update your account telephone number, I inputed the home phone and your cell phone numbers into the computer, and when you called, it showed your name on the Caller ID. I see you're calling from your home phone."

Bingo. A man had gone to the store posing as Augustus Grant and managed to get the clerk to give him Becca Itoh's home phone number. He'd probably given some story about wanting to make sure the number was correct, and if the clerk could please tell him what the number on file was.

Shaun spoke up. "Hi there, we're on speakerphone. I have a question for you. Do you have videotape surveillance at your store?"

"Oh, yes. We're very conscious of security because of the many hard-to-find videos at our store. We have a closed-circuit system and we keep the videotapes for up to a month."

"That's great," Shaun said. "We're going to need to come by to look at those."

"You will?" The girl's voice rose. "Why?"

"Because you gave this telephone number to a man posing as Augustus Grant."

The girl was silent a long moment, then began sputtering. "Oh, my goodness. I'm so sorry...."

"It's fine," Monica rushed in to assure her. "But if you could show us the video so we can see who got the telephone number, that would be very helpful to us."

"Certainly. Of course. I'm so sorry...."

"Thank you. We'll be by shortly." Monica hung up and then glared at Shaun. "Did you have to phrase it like that? The poor girl is traumatized."

"She shouldn't have given out your home phone number without even asking to see a driver's license," Shaun said. "Besides, since she now realizes she did something wrong, she'll be likely to let us look at the video surveillance without questioning us."

Monica again insisted on driving and they went to the DVD rental store in downtown Sonoma. The day was overcast today, but no rain, and a cold wind blew them into the store.

A young nervous woman stood behind the register, pale and slender. She bit her lip as they approached. "Er...Can I help you?"

"My name is Monica Grant, and this is my...associate, Shaun O'Neill. We spoke on the phone."

"You're not Ms. Itoh." The girl's brown eyes were wide like a deer.

"Becca Itoh is my aunt."

Shaun nudged Monica even as he reached into his back pocket for his wallet. "Show her your driver's license and those bills I told you to bring."

Monica pulled everything out of her purse. "My driver's license still has my San Francisco apartment number, but I've been living at home for the past year and a half." She produced bills with her name and the home address on them. "Check this address with the one you have on file for Becca Itoh. I also have a credit card with the same number my aunt used, but my card has my name on it, so you can check the credit card number you have on file with my card."

It took almost fifteen minutes before the girl had verified they were who they said they were. Shaun supposed it was his fault for scaring her with the telephone call.

"Now," he said, leaning against the counter. "We want to know who you gave the Grants' home phone number to."

Her gaze darted between him and Monica. "Uh...shouldn't I tell this to the police?"

"You can tell them, too, but first you're going to show us the surveillance video so we can see what he looks like."

"It's very important," Monica said gently. "The man used that telephone number to call and threaten me."

The girl swallowed hard. "It's in back. I'll get my boss to show you." She led them through a door in the wall, which opened into a small staff room with another door on the other side.

She knocked tentatively until a gruff voice said, "What is it, Natalie?"

"Uncle Randy, I have a couple of customers here who need to talk to you."

The door opened to a tall, very slender man with wispy gray-brown hair. He peered at them through his silver-framed glasses. "How can I help you?"

"A man posed as my father," Monica said, "and manipulated Natalie into giving him our home telephone number."

The way she'd phrased it made it not sound like Natalie had so blithely given away their information. Natalie's head was down, though, obviously embarrassed and anxious about her mistake.

Randy frowned at his niece. "You did?"

"I'm sorry, Uncle Randy. He knew a lot about Ms. Itoh, making it seem that he was who he said he was."

"It might actually turn out to be a good thing," Monica said quickly, "because Natalie said that you have video surveillance in the store. We've been trying to get a picture of this man."

"Yes, the videos are here." Randy stepped aside so they could enter his office. It was a large room, with his desk on one side and on the other side a wall unit with two televisions and the recording equipment. Randy sat at a chair in front of the wall unit and brought up the video archive feed. "When did this happen?"

"Five days ago," Natalie said.

The video feed appeared in one of the TV screens, and he fast-forwarded it until Natalie said, "There."

He played the video at normal speed, and it showed a tall man with a very large protruding stomach and even less hair than Randy.

Definitely not Phillip.

"Who is that?" Monica asked.

"You don't know?" he asked.

"I've never seen him before in my life."

Was this the stalker? But people had described an average man, average height. The man in the video was very tall and balding. He could have worn a wig, perhaps, but he couldn't have disguised his height.

"He said he was Augustus Grant," Natalie said, "and that Ms. Itoh was his sister-in-law. Ms. Itoh is one of our best customers, and he knew her address, and where she worked. He said that she'd sent him to make sure we had the right telephone number on file for the house. I had a home phone and a cell phone. He told me the home phone number was correct but the cell phone number was wrong, and he gave me a new one."

Shaun reached into his pocket for his cell phone. "What number did he give you?"

Natalie went out to the computer behind the register to get the phone number, and when she gave it to Shaun, he dialed it.

It went to a disconnected number.

"Did you read off Becca's cell phone number to him, too?" Shaun asked.

Natalie shook her head quickly. "I only gave the first few digits and he said that it was wrong, and gave me the new one."

"But you read off the entire number for the home phone."

Natalie's eyes fell to the floor as she nodded.

It would make the man seem a bit more legitimate, Shaun supposed, if he didn't ask her to read off both numbers to him entirely. His interrupting her seemed more natural.

Whoever this guy was, he was good.

"Could we take this video to the police?" Monica asked. "They might be able to find out who this man is."

"Sure," Randy said. "Anything to help." He popped the DVD out of the player and gave it to them. "I'm sorry again, folks. It won't happen again."

"We know," Monica said. "Thanks."

Detective Carter wasn't at the police station when they went to drop off the DVD, but Monica left a note for him with an officer who promised to make sure he looked at it when he returned. Shaun had also made an MP3 file of the conversation with the stalker and left that for the detective.

"I guess it's kind of silly of me to think my case is his only priority," Monica said as they were driving back to the Grants' home.

Shaun glanced in the rearview mirror and stilled.

The old Honda Accord a few cars behind them had been behind them on the way to the police station.

It could be coincidence. The driver had gone somewhere near the police station, then left around the same time they did, on this street which was a major one into and out of downtown.

Or maybe it wasn't the same Accord. The one he'd seen had been the same color—grayish silver from age and sun fading, well-worn and very dusty. This one seemed the same, but he couldn't be entirely sure. Old Honda Accords weren't common, but they weren't rare, either.

Monica picked up on his concern. "What is it?"

"I'm not sure." He didn't want to alarm her, but... "Take four left turns."

"Are we being followed?" She gave a quick glance in her rearview mirror.

"I don't know. Let's find out."

For once he was almost glad he wasn't driving, because he was able to keep his eye on the Accord and try to get a license plate number or a look at the driver. All he saw was a shadowy figure who wore sunglasses.

"Drive normally," he told Monica. "Not too fast. If there is someone tailing us, you don't want to let him know we're on to him."

She tapped her fingers on the steering wheel, but her face was calm. "I want to draw him out."

"No heroics. Remember what your aunt told you."

Monica took a left turn onto a side street. "I've known he had to be tailing my car for the past few weeks, or else he couldn't have known where I'd be. But this is the first time we might actually see him there."

"I'll look. You keep your eyes on the road."

She took another left turn. "Can you see him?"

Shaun shook his head. "When you turned, he hadn't yet made the first left turn."

"Maybe we're not being followed."

Somehow, he doubted that.

She took two more left turns, but the Accord didn't appear behind them. They were finally back on the main road and he scanned the cars behind them. No Accord. Maybe they hadn't been followed. Maybe it was all in his head.

No, he had to keep his head in the game. He couldn't afford to slip up with this guy.

Then, as they were nearing the edge of town, he saw it, gleaming dully in the overcast light, several cars behind them.

He turned back around in his seat and looked at where they were. They'd been safer in the middle of the town, but now they were heading out into open countryside. It was too deserted. "Can you get back to town?"

"Is he there?" Her voice had a wobbly edge to it.

"We don't want to get to a lonely stretch of road. Can you turn around somewhere?" There were vineyards on either side of the road and narrow strips of grass for the shoulder.

"We're not out of town yet, so there are still lots of cars. I'd have to pull over and wait for a break in traffic to pull a U-turn."

No, he didn't want them to be stopped on the side of the road and unable to turn. "Where else can you turn?"

"A mile or two up ahead is a stoplight. I can slow down as I get there and try to gun through before it turns red. If he's far enough behind us, he'll be stuck at the stoplight."

"But we'd be getting farther out into the countryside. We need to get back to town."

"If that doesn't work, I can turn right at Olson's Crossing. It's a road that loops around Farmer Olson's property and shoots you back out onto the main road again. We can head back to town then."

"Okay, let's do it."

As she drove, he had a fleeting thought that here was the

perfect opportunity to catch this man, to lure him out, to find out once and for all who he was. But his desire to capture the stalker warred with his desire to protect Monica only for a second—Monica came first.

"Here we go." She slowed the car down as they started to approach a stoplight ahead. It regulated a three-way intersection.

"Don't get us stuck at the light," Shaun said.

"Trust me."

In a strange way, he did. But trust her driving? That was another matter.

Cars behind her started to honk. She ignored them and kept a slow pace as she approached the light.

Green turned yellow.

She slowed down even more.

Her lips were moving, and Shaun realized she was counting.

"Six," she said. Then gunned the engine.

Her car shot through the intersection just as the light turned red. The car next in line behind her didn't have time to accelerate and coast through the intersection with her, and was stuck at the light.

With the Accord three cars behind.

She let out a long breath and leaned back in her seat. Her hands were shaking slightly.

"How did you do that?" Shaun asked.

"In high school, my friends and I would play pranks on each other. We'd purposely try to leave each other at the light. I got good at counting and knowing when to accelerate."

They rode in silence for a while, then she said, "We should have tried to get a better look at him."

"No," Shaun said firmly. "He's angry. We don't know what he'd do."

Then he looked back and saw the Accord. Accelerating fast.

"He's found us," Shaun said. "He must have passed the other cars in front of him. Your car is faster. You can lose him."

"But in a few yards, the road becomes winding," Monica said. "We'll be on equal footing."

"Is there anywhere to turn?" High banks edged the road now, along with some pine trees.

"No, but the winding part only lasts a mile or two, then becomes straight. I can outrun him."

If they got there.

She took the first curve too fast, and her tires squealed.

"Don't crash," he said.

"Let me do the driving," she said. "You see if you can see his face."

The Accord's dirty windshield masked the driver's features. All Saun could see was the dark shadows on the man's sunglasses. There was no license plate on the front of the car.

As she took turn after turn, Shaun realized that she did know her car better than he did, and she pushed the car to its limit on each curve. She took them at alarming speeds, but she never lost control of the car. The Accord began to drop back.

They shot out into a long stretch of open road, but then she started to slow down.

"What are you doing?" Shaun demanded.

"I know what I'm doing." She kept glancing in the rearview mirror.

The Accord appeared behind them and Shaun heard the old engine grind and roar as the man sped up after them.

"He's gaining on us."

"Good," she said.

Closer. Closer. Still Monica slowed down her car.

"He's going to hit us!" Shaun said.

"No, he's not!" Monica sharply pulled the car to one side of the road and hit the brakes.

She'd been going slow enough that the car didn't veer out of control, but the Accord scraped the side with a shriek of metal as it shot past them. Shaun felt the steel vibrations in his teeth.

He also remembered to look at the rear license plate number: 2PSK0 something.

Monica then turned the car around in a tight U-turn on the narrow road and shot back the way they'd come.

"I can lose him again in the winding part," she said.

Shaun turned and saw only the taillights behind them. "I don't think he's going to try to follow us. He's driving away."

She executed the winding stretch of road at a slightly slower speed, and they kept their eyes open behind them for the Accord, but it never appeared again.

"I owe you an apology," Shaun said.

"For what?"

"You definitely can drive defensively. Maybe even better than me."

She gave him a dry sidelong look. "It also helped that I once dated a race car driver."

EIGHT

A few days later, Monica tried not to look around as she and Shaun walked down the street toward Lorianne's Café. "Are we being followed?"

"I don't know."

Her entire back tingled, and she could almost feel the stalker's eyes on her.

"Slow down," Shaun said. "If you walk too quickly, you'll look nervous."

They had to look normal. They couldn't do anything to make the stalker think anything was wrong. Not just yet.

They entered the restaurant, and Lorianne met them with a serious expression rather than her typical hug for Monica. "I hope you know what you're doing."

Monica hoped so, too.

They followed Lorianne, who sat them at a table in the middle of the dining area—not too close to the window, but not too far in the back where someone spying on the restaurant from outside couldn't see Monica and Shaun sitting down.

"All right, here I go." Monica got up, leaving her purse, and headed to the women's restroom.

Her sister Naomi met her just inside the door. "For the record, I think this is too dangerous."

"For you or for me?" Monica shed the bright white coat she'd worn and helped Naomi to put it on.

"For you, of course," Naomi said.

"All we need is for you and Shaun's brother Brady to pose as us for a few minutes. Just long enough for us to sneak out the back and lose him."

"We don't look that much alike." Naomi pulled out a dark wig from a tote bag she'd brought with her, and Monica helped her adjust it on her head.

"You don't need to look exactly like me, just close enough that someone couldn't tell from a distance."

"What if he comes inside the restaurant?"

"Shaun thinks he probably will. But by the time he manages to get a look at you and realizes it's not me, we'll be gone and he won't have a clue where we went." Monica helped her shove her light brown hair up under the dark tresses of the wig. "Keep your eyes open. You might get a look at him."

Naomi tugged at the wig. "Aunt Becca said you've been getting more pictures."

Monica nodded. "Every day. He sends photos he took a few days earlier." After following them a few days ago, it appeared he'd continued to follow them in the days since. She shivered a little. She could almost feel the heat of his anger as she flouted his command for her to stop work on the clinic.

"Okay, you look close enough." She looked at the two of them in the bathroom mirror. Monica and Naomi had always looked the most alike of the three sisters, although Naomi had a rounder face and hazel eyes, and Monica had darker hair and clear amber eyes.

Naomi exited the women's restroom, which wasn't visible from the windows or doors at the front of the restaurant, and went to sit in Monica's chair. Monica slipped out of the restroom and headed through the kitchens to sneak out the back of the restaurant. Everyone was busy and no one paid her much attention, but she scrutinized each face. Would the stalker have already snuck into the restaurant posed as one of the staff? Or would she meet him at the back door on her way out?

The thought made her hesitate before the back door, but then she felt a tall presence behind her and whirled around.

It was Shaun. "Let's go." He pushed the door open.

The alley in the back of the restaurant was empty, and they headed down to a side street where Shaun's brother Brady had parked his SUV. At this moment, Brady was having lunch with Naomi in Shaun's place.

"Did you get as much of an earful as I did?" Shaun asked her.

"They're just worried about us."

"I still don't think this is a great idea." They reached the SUV, parked on a deserted side street, and Shaun unlocked the doors.

"We're not doing anything reckless." Monica got into the passenger seat.

"We're playing cloak and dagger with our siblings."

"Do you really want the stalker to follow us as we visit the private investigator he hired to get my phone number?" Monica demanded. "I'm sure my stalker would be thrilled to let us talk to John Butler."

"Detective Carter got nothing from Butler." Shaun started the engine and looked over his shoulder before pulling away from the curb. "What makes you think you can do any better?"

Monica fished the sunglasses she'd stowed in her pocket and slipped them on, in case the stalker caught a glimpse of her driving past him. "I don't have high expectations. But I have to at least talk to him, maybe make him understand that his client is stalking me. Put a face to the name of that telephone number he acquired." Maybe appeal to his softer side, to tell them where to find his client.

She had to try.

They drove out of Sonoma and headed into San Francisco, then farther south to Daly City. Detective Carter had reluctantly given Monica the name of the man he'd identified from the surveillance video at the DVD rental store, but she knew the detective had been forced to do it because she had the right to press charges. It didn't escape her that Detective Carter told her about John Butler only after he'd already spoken to the private investigator.

Shaun and Monica had both immediately realized that Butler's client must be her stalker.

The section of town that Butler's office was located in had a dingy gray film over everything—the buildings, the cars, the street, even the sky looked more overcast. They parked on the street in front of a tiny Chinese bakery with iron bars over the front windows, and entered a door to the side of the bakery that had a crooked sign that read, John Butler, Private Investigator.

The door opened into a narrow hallway and a steep flight of concrete stairs. They climbed the stairs to the apartment above the bakery and knocked on a wooden door with faded green paint peeling off it in strips.

Heavy footsteps sounded, then a pause as Butler looked through his peephole. The pause was so long, Monica wondered if maybe he'd been warned she was coming and wouldn't open the door to them. She raised her hand to knock again, but the door cracked open.

"Can I help you?"

Not very friendly for a man greeting potential customers.

"John Butler?" She tried to put on a warm smile, but it felt sickly on her lips. "My name is—"

"I know who you are." His beady black eyes narrowed, making his round face appear even larger.

"I just wanted you to meet me," she said. "I wanted you to see the woman your client is stalking." She used the word deliberately, to try to shock him into any sort of reaction, but the only reaction she got was a snort of derision.

"Yeah, yeah. You can tell me any story you want, it'll still be what my client says versus what you say."

"Don't you even care that he's threatened her life?" Shaun growled. "He tried to ram her car a few days ago."

"He obviously didn't succeed, which means you're either a race car driver or he wasn't trying too hard." Butler's thick red lips sneered at them.

"Please," Monica said. "Won't you let us come inside? Let me explain—"

"You can talk right where you're standing," Butler replied. "And it doesn't mean I have to listen."

"This man is trying to kill me," Monica said. "And he already killed Shaun's sister. Please just tell us who he is so he won't hurt any more women."

His mouth tightened for a moment, and he blinked once. Then the sharpness returned to his black eyes and he said, "I couldn't tell you if I wanted to. He told me his name was John Smith, and he paid in cash."

Monica bit her lip. Of course he had.

"When was this?" Shaun asked.

"He came to me about three weeks ago. Wanted your address, phone number, all that. I found your San Francisco info first but he wanted your Sonoma address."

Something squirmed inside her at the thought of this man and the stalker finding out her personal information so easily, in only a few weeks.

"What did he look like?" Shaun asked.

"Average," Butler said impatiently. "Brown hair, brown

eyes, big nose. Eyes close together. Look, are we done? I was up all night doing surveillance."

Monica pulled out her business card, the one she'd had made for the free children's clinic, and then realized it had her cell phone number. If she'd met the stalker at the Zoe banquet and talked to him about the clinic, he already had her business card and her cell phone number. The stalker had deliberately wanted Butler to get her home phone number, the one that was harder to find, in order to intimidate her more.

"If you think of anything else, please call me," she said to Butler.

He grunted, but took her card.

Shaun also gave him his business card, and then Butler closed the door in their faces without even saying goodbye.

The stairs seemed longer and steeper on the way down. All this way for nothing. She'd thought Butler might have been a little kinder toward the end of the brief conversation, but he was still a hard-nosed businessman with questionable morals. He didn't care enough to want to help her.

On the drive back to Sonoma, she said, "Now it all seems silly—asking Naomi and Brady to switch places with us, driving all this way."

"We got a description," Shaun said.

"We got lots of descriptions from all those other people we talked to."

"But this was a P.I. They're not bystander eyewitnesses. Their business is paying attention to faces and details. Butler wasn't very descriptive, but his picture of the stalker matches a couple other people we talked to."

"Average. Brown hair and eyes, big nose, close-set eyes."

"It's better than nothing. And just because this is a dead end doesn't mean we don't have any other leads."

She realized he was right. "The investors I talked to at the

Zoe banquet. But what are we going to do, interview all of them and see if they smell like cigarette smoke?"

Shaun sighed. "No, that's out. I don't want you talking to the potential stalker. It's possible to hide cigarette smoke, anyway. Dad used to smoke pipes a lot when we were younger. He had a corduroy jacket he wore whenever he smoked outside in the garden. The jacket smelled like smoke but he didn't."

But Monica's head was whirling with ideas. "I still think we can eliminate some of the investors. The stalker has been taking pictures of me every day, now. I get an envelope in the mail every morning, and the photos inside were taken from a few days before."

He glanced at her. "What does that have to do with the investors?"

"If he's taking pictures of me, he can't be meeting with me at the same time."

Shaun hesitated before saying, "You mean, you want to arrange meetings with the people you met at the Zoe banquet, and then see if the stalker takes pictures of you with them? No way."

"It could work. If there aren't any pictures of me with a particular investor, that might be our guy. We could figure out who he is by process of elimination."

She could tell he was tempted. It would be a strategy that would bring them closer to the stalker's identity without bringing her any closer to the stalker than she already was every day with the guy taking pictures of her everywhere she went.

Shaun shook his head. "You don't think he'd think of that, once you start calling and making appointments with investors?"

"But it doesn't mean he knows who I met at the Zoe banquet. The people I talk to in the next few days could simply be investors I met at a number of other events."

"It's dangerous."

"Me not stopping work on this clinic is dangerous. My party next week is dangerous. Do you really want to just let him go so he could stalk some other woman rather than taking this opportunity of finding out who he is?"

"There's no guarantee this'll work."

"You're right." She sat back in her seat. "But don't you think it's worth a shot? Right now he's taking pictures of me every day, and we don't know how long he's going to continue doing this. What might happen is that he realizes too late that he can't take pictures of himself when he's with me, but by then we'll have eliminated a few investors."

She also wanted this challenge of looking him in the eye and seeing if she could tell he was her stalker. A part of her wanted to prove to herself that she could still read people as well as she always did, that this guy couldn't hide his true nature from her. She'd met him once before and been clueless. Now she wanted a rematch.

Yes, that was childish of her. But it felt like the only thing she could control in this entire situation. Everything else was being done to manipulate her, and she hated it.

"What do you say?" she asked Shaun. "We can have all the meetings in public places, and you'll be nearby."

He sighed. "It's not as if I could stop you."

"But I want to know you support me in this, that you'll protect me."

The look he sent her way was brief but intense, and it made her skin prickle. "I'll always protect you."

Yes, she knew he would.

She both did and didn't want to provoke the stalker again. Once he saw her talking to more investors, he would be livid.

Would he escalate to violence once it became obvious she wasn't going to be intimidated?

Because she refused to be intimidated. She refused to be told what to do by a man mentally and emotionally unstable.

"Let's do it," she said with a firm nod. "Let's flush him out."

Two down, four to go.

Out of all the investors Monica had spoken to at the Zoe banquet, only six had come close to the description of the stalker—male, brown hair, average height. She'd called all of them to arrange meetings, leaving voicemails for four of them, but she'd spoken to the other two and had arranged meetings with them yesterday. She'd made sure it wasn't hard for the stalker to follow her, and she had brief meetings with the two investors at an outdoor café in San Francisco.

Today was number three, Brett Marshall.

She'd received more photos this morning, but she was almost glad to get them because they meant that in a few days, she'd be able to see if photos of the investors began showing up.

It gave her a sense of power, to be deliberately putting herself in the stalker's camera rather than wanting to hide from it. It made her feel more in control.

Brett had mentioned he wanted to meet at his restaurant there, so Monica and Shaun drove to Napa in his Chevy Suburban, a gigantic tank of an SUV. Her car was with the police as evidence—being sidelined by the stalker's vehicle had left some paint scraped along her driver's side door.

Her cell phone rang, and she saw Jason Mars's ID pop up. One of the other investors had mentioned that Jason was very tight with his money, and that even if he expressed interest in the project, he rarely ever gave to a charity that didn't somehow benefit his business, so she was surprised he'd called her back. "Hello."

"Monica, it's Jason Mars. I got your message. Yes, I got your invitation to the party. I'm not sure yet if I'll be attending." He was curt and to the point.

"I was hoping I could meet with you to discuss my purpose for the party and the free children's clinic. I'd be happy to answer any questions you might have."

"I can meet with you today if you're free. I've been busy chasing down bank managers who won't return my calls."

Of all the investors, she had disliked talking to him the most. His conversation seemed to focus on injustices he'd had to face or bad luck that had fallen on him or people who had betrayed him.

Aside from his negativity, she had also had the feeling that he'd been holding back some deep-seated anger. Or maybe it had just been anger at the world and feeling life was unfair.

"I'm afraid I can't meet with you today," Monica said. "I'm in Napa. I have a meeting at Rock Love restaurant."

He suddenly grew quiet, and Monica could almost hear his temper simmering. What had she said to upset him? The only thing she could think of was that he also owned a restaurant, Elementals, but it seemed petty for him to be upset about that, especially since Elementals was in Marin.

"Rock Love?" His voice sounded strangled. "Brett Marshall's restaurant?"

"I didn't realize you two were rivals. Elementals is entirely different cuisine from Rock Love."

"I've never been to Rock Love, so I wouldn't know. I wouldn't step foot in his restaurant if you paid me. Brett Marshall doesn't respect women and will try to rip you off and take everything from you."

His harsh tone surprised her as much as his confusing words. However, she didn't want to gossip and she also didn't want to walk smack dab in the center of some feud between the two men. "Why don't I arrange to meet with you tomorrow?"

"Is Brett who you're meeting?" Jason persisted. "You're meeting with Brett?"

"I'm sure you understand that it would be unprofessional for me to tell you who I'm meeting. Many of my investors appreciate their anonymity."

"You're a fool if you let him invest in your clinic."

She couldn't help but think that she couldn't exactly write Brett off just on Jason's word, especially when Brett had expressed more genuine interest in investing in the clinic than Jason had.

But his animosity both startled and puzzled her. There again was that deep-seated anger she'd noticed the first time she spoke to him. Coupled with his negative worldview, would he want to threaten her to make her stop work on her clinic, perhaps for some obscure reason only he knew about? Would he have done the same to Clare and killed her?

And yet her gut told her that he wasn't the stalker. He definitely seemed to have some issues, but Monica had a hard time believing that a man like Jason Mars, who couldn't hide his anger toward Brett, would be able to hide his hatred of the clinic from her when speaking about it. He also hadn't been angry when talking about the party, and the stalker had been wildly upset about that.

"Jason, if you'd like, I can have lunch with you tomorrow at some place near your office. Your center of operations is in San Francisco, isn't it?"

"I'll have to check with my schedule and get back to you," he said, and hung up.

Jason wasn't the rudest man she'd ever encountered, but he did seem to rub her the wrong way.

They entered downtown Napa and found Brett's restaurant, Rock Love. With a name like Rock Love, Monica had expected rock band memorabilia or a music theme, but instead the decor was in rough-hewn textures in shades of brown, beige, gray and black with chrome accents. The only spots of color were the bottles of drinks behind the extensive bar. Monica realized the name referred to a rock-climbing theme, not rock 'n' roll.

Brett met them as they walked in the front double doors, which were trapezoid shaped and very flashy from the outside. He had wavy brown hair and a wide forehead that made his eyes seem more close-set than they actually were. He had a classic Roman nose but sensual lips and a flirtatious manner that somehow made a woman seem appreciated. Of all the investors, he looked the most like Phillip Bromley, and yet his personality was the polar opposite. Whereas Phillip seemed self-serving and secretive, Brett was open and even blunt at times.

"Monica, your beautiful face brightens this entire place." Brett leaned forward to kiss her, but she turned her head to the side so he kissed her cheek instead.

"Brett, you're so sweet. This is Shaun, he drove me here. I hope you don't mind putting him at a table near us?"

"Of course." He signaled to the hostess, who looked at her computer to figure out a table to put Shaun. The restaurant was already filled with people for lunch, mostly tourists and a few businesspeople, although Rock Love had a reputation for having a more raucous crowd in the evening.

Brett led her to a booth in the corner of the restaurant, but on the way there, several of his customers stood up to chat with him.

"Mr. Marshall, I just wanted to say what a great place you've got here," said one man.

"Thanks. Hey, what are you eating?" Brett asked him.

"We haven't decided yet."

"The salmon's a little oily today, but the black cod is the best I've tasted yet."

"Thanks, Mr. Marshall."

In watching Brett take the time to talk to these people, Monica was reminded of her first impression of him at the Zoe banquet—he was personable and yet he spoke directly and as without pretense as he could.

They finally got to their booth and Brett stood aside while Monica scooted in. However, he sat uncomfortably close to her, so she moved over and put her purse between them.

The hostess approached with Shaun trailing behind, but the table she seated him at was several yards away. The other tables nearby were already filled, so she supposed she shouldn't be surprised, but without his presence, she felt cold and isolated.

"I hope you don't mind, but I ordered drinks for us." Brett signaled a waiter, who arrived seconds later with a bottle of champagne.

"I am so very sorry, but I'm afraid I don't drink alcohol during meetings. It's a personal stance I take," she said.

He took it smoothly. "Well, then, maybe after lunch." His lips curved as if they hid some playful secret, while his eyes seemed to be drinking her in.

"You suggested the black cod?" Monica picked up her menu and glanced at it. "I have to admit I've been wanting to try your restaurant for some time, but just never had an excuse to come to Napa for lunch."

He smiled slowly and draped his arm over the back of the seat. "I'm glad I'm your excuse," he said in a low voice.

Brett wasn't unattractive, but his seductive flirting didn't appeal to her. He made her feel like just the next woman he was interested in.

She couldn't help comparing how Brett made her feel with how Shaun made her feel. Shaun's protectiveness and concern for her made her feel special to him, like an honor only rarely given to women in his life. The way he spoke to her, even the way he kissed her, seemed to tell her that she was significant to him, not just a blip in his love life.

"Monica, I'll lay my cards on the table," Brett said. "I'm very attracted to you. I was from the moment I saw you. I was in London on business the week after the Zoe banquet or I would have called you, but when I got the invitation to your party, I knew I had to see you before then."

Rather than making her feel more uncomfortable, his honesty impressed her. His tendency to be a straight-shooter was such a rarity among all the investors she had met. She appreciated it, and she regretted that she might hurt his feelings by rebuffing him. "Brett, I'm very flattered. But I have to admit that I just don't feel the same way about you."

"Are you sure?" Brett leaned a little closer, and she smelled the spicy green scent of his soap. Somehow he didn't smell as manly as Shaun. She cast a quick look in Shaun's direction and met his glower.

Brett continued, "I know you're not repulsed by me, at least."

She'd be as honest with him as he was with her. "Yes, you are an attractive man, but I'm not emotionally attracted to you, if that makes sense."

Something flickered in his eyes—surprise, maybe. Respect, definitely.

Monica continued, "And if you decide not to support the clinic as a result, I'm willing to face that consequence. But I won't string you along for the sake of the clinic. It's not honest and it's unprofessional."

His smile was brighter than any he'd shown to her before. "I'd be lying if I said I wasn't disappointed, but I have to tell you, you're a woman in a million. I respect you even more now, if that's possible."

The way he took her rejection didn't surprise her. He gave the impression that he valued honesty over other things in his life, even his romantic interests.

"Did you still want to continue?" She phrased it calmly, but inside she was quaking. Would she lose this man as an investor? He'd been one of her most promising leads, and also one of the most influential.

"Most definitely." He picked up her hand and kissed it, then winked at her. "I'm not flirting with you, I promise. I think you will be a joy to work with, Miss Grant."

"Then let's order so we can get started."

As she made her presentation for the clinic, Brett asked intelligent questions and had a keen understanding of some of the problems she might come up with, but without having a wet blanket attitude about the project.

Occasionally she'd look toward Shaun's table, and each time found him watching her like a hawk. His intense scrutiny should have annoyed her, but instead, it somehow made her feel looked after. No other man in her life had treated her this way, as if she were precious.

"I don't think he's just your driver." Brett gestured toward Shaun with his head.

"He's my bodyguard," she admitted.

"You need protection? Why? From whom?"

"Nothing really serious. There's some opposition to this free children's clinic." She hoped it sounded innocuous enough.

"There's always a few of them," Brett said. "I had people who didn't want me to build this restaurant. But I also have a lot of people who enjoy eating here and working here. It makes it worth it, in the end."

He was right. She believed in her children's clinic, and it would be worth all this stress and emotional energy when she could open the clinic doors and treat her first patient.

A blur of movement caught her eye and she suddenly saw Jason Mars barreling through the restaurant right toward them.

Jason had a square face and piggish eyes set close to his large red nose. His hair a curly brown, but thinning near the top, and his ears stuck out from his face. His skin had a tendency toward redness, and he was the same color as a cherry soda at the moment.

"I knew it," Jason raged at her. "I knew you were meeting him."

Her seated position, even though she was behind the table, made her feel vulnerable, but when she would have moved out of the booth to stand up to face Jason, Brett put a hand on her arm to stop her.

"You had to insist on ignoring me," Jason continued. "You couldn't just take some well-meaning advice. You women are all the same."

"That's uncalled for, Mars," Brett said.

"What do you care? You just want to make money."

"That's the pot calling the kettle black, isn't it?" Brett responded dryly.

Suddenly, two waiters who were a bit taller and broader than the others approached Jason. "Sir, we'd like you to come with us."

"No." Brett waved them back. "Let him say what he wants to say. I have no secrets."

"You lying snake!" Spittle from Jason's mouth flew over the table. "How dare you say that after what you did to my marriage?"

"I didn't do anything to your marriage." Brett's expression was as stone cold as his voice. "You're the one who left your wife."

Monica hadn't known that. When had that happened?

"You're the one who seduced her away from me!" Jason said.

Monica could feel Jason's anger rolling out of him like a sandstorm, wiping everything out of its way including reason and logic. It had nothing to do with her, no matter what Jason might have told himself, and she wanted to escape its path.

She turned toward Shaun's table, but he was gone. Had he gone to the restroom, or stepped outside to take a phone call? She knew he wouldn't abandon her. She just had to wait for him.

"You're trying to take me down," Jason told Brett. "You're trying to run me out of business and destroy my marriage, tear apart my family."

"That's ridiculous." Brett lost control of his calm facade and rolled his eyes. "I opened a few successful restaurants that don't even cater to the same clientele as yours. I'm not gunning for you. And all I did was be kind to your wife and offer her a ride home from a party."

Jason's face glowed as red as coals. "That's how you start it, with rides home. Then you seduce them away from men who really love them. Well, let me return the favor."

He darted forward, faster than Monica would have expected from such a stout man, and reached across the table to grab her arm in a beefy hand. He gripped her so hard that she thought her humerus bone might bend beneath his fingers, and she cried out in pain.

"Hey!" Brett shouted at him. He and the two waiters descended on Jason. Brett grabbed Jason's other shoulder, and the waiters tried to grab him around the upper arm and the back of his jacket, but Jason still had a tight hold on Monica, so they couldn't pull him away without hurting her.

Then a different hand clamped around Jason's wrist. Monica looked up and saw that Shaun had circled around Jason and the waiters to the other side of the booth, next to her.

Shaun's thumb pressed Jason's ulnar nerve against the

bone, causing him excruciating pain. His hand around Monica's arm loosened, and Shaun forced him away from her. The two waiters pulled him back, immobilizing his arms.

"You're not welcome in my restaurant, Mr. Mars." Brett's voice was taut.

"I'm never investing in your clinic," Jason ranted at Monica.

"That's good," Brett replied, "because as of right now, I'm committing to investing in it. Unlike you, I think that Sonoma county needs a free children's medical clinic." He turned to Monica. "Did you want to press charges?"

"No."

He nodded to the waiters, who hauled Jason out of the dining room. Then Brett stood and raised his voice to calmly address the other diners. "I'm so sorry about that, folks..."

A light touch on her shoulder made her turn and meet Shaun's fierce blue eyes.

"Are you all right?" he asked.

"I'm fine, thanks to you."

His finger lifted and gently touched her jawline. That one soft point of contact burned against her skin. Then he removed his hand from her shoulder and stepped away.

She scooted out of the booth and rose to her feet. Her knees shook, but her loose business slacks hid it.

Brett turned to her. "I'm really sorry."

"No, I am. He wouldn't have known I was here if I hadn't let it slip when I was talking to him on the phone a couple hours ago."

"Did he hurt you?"

"No. But I hope he didn't hurt your restaurant or your reputation." Even if Jason's accusations were false, the gossip could spread like wildfire.

Brett surprised her with his grin. "Are you kidding? There were several people shooting video with their phones. It'll be on the internet in a few hours. The publicity will be fantastic for this restaurant. There's no such thing as bad publicity."

"I understand if you weren't serious about investing in the clinic," Monica said. "I don't want you to invest just on the spur of the moment."

Brett laughed. "I'd committed to investing while you were giving your presentation, but…" He lifted a cautionary finger. "…provided I can also look at your business plan before I sign anything."

"Of course. All the investors will be getting a copy as soon as it's finalized. Thank you." She reached into the booth to collect her purse.

"I can't interest you in dessert?" Brett said ruefully.

"I'm afraid I have to get back to Sonoma," Monica said. "I have to take my dad to his physical therapy session this afternoon."

"Well, I'll look forward to the party, then." Brett shook her hand and leaned forward to kiss her again, but he bussed her cheek without her even needing to turn her head.

Shaun's face seemed to have a cloud over it as he walked her out of the restaurant, and he didn't look at her. Jealous. He was jealous. The thought made her heart give a quick leap.

No.

She rubbed her hand against her breastbone to make the warm feeling go away. After they caught this stalker, Shaun would apply for the Sonoma Police Department. She had to remember that.

They exited the restaurant, but the sudden roar of a car engine sent her pulse hammering in her ears. At the same moment, Shaun thrust an arm out in front of her and positioned his body as a shield.

From their right, a car shot toward them.

They backpedaled a few steps, Monica clinging to Shaun's arm. There was a loud buzzing in her ears from the adrenaline.

A shiny silver sports car came to a halt in front of them, and Jason Mars leaned out the open driver's side window. His face was ugly and his eyes wide and wild.

"You'll regret this," he growled.

Then he stepped on the gas and drove away.

NINE

It had been four days since Monica's first meeting with investors, and no photos had arrived from the stalker.

Shaun wondered if he'd been expecting the guy to be too stupid or arrogant to realize what Monica was doing, but it looked like he might have caught on to the trap they'd laid for him.

The only photos Shaun had seen had been shots of the argument taken by diners at Brett Marshall's restaurant, along with a couple of videos posted on the web. Like Marshall had predicted, the argument had gotten him a lot of publicity for his restaurant. However, it didn't seem to have caught the stalker's attention.

What did that mean? Was the stalker silent about the argument and the attack on Monica because either Marshall or Mars was the stalker? Wouldn't the stalker revel in the fact that one of Monica's investors hurt her?

It had been all he could do not to rise up to punch Jason Mars in the chin for grabbing Monica. He'd also had to rein himself when Marshall had flirted with her all through lunch. Rock Love was supposed to be an award-winning restaurant, but the food had been ashes in his mouth.

"Are you almost done?" she asked him.

He pulled his mind back to what he was supposed to be

doing, which was setting up the video camera for her computer so she could video chat with one of her investors, Rodney Lassiter.

Monica had mentioned that Lassiter was very young—only twenty-five years old—but already VP of his family's successful luxury foods distribution company. He had been in college in Boston while Clare was in L.A. But he was about Phillip's height, although his hair was a lighter brown, so she'd left a message for him when she called the other investors from the Zoe banquet that they suspected might be the stalker. Lassiter had called her a couple of days ago to set up this video chat appointment because he was supposedly in Florida.

Shaun watched her put finishing touches on her makeup and straighten the collar of her conservative business suit. She was beautiful, as always, but he preferred her more casual clothes when she was with him a few days ago and they were trying to figure out where the stalker had been when taking each of the photos he'd sent to her. She'd had on jeans and a blouse, and her dark hair had waved around her face and down her shoulders. He'd wanted to touch it. He'd wanted to touch her neck, her jaw, her cheek.

He closed his eyes and shook his head. He had to stop this.

Who was he kidding? His reaction to Monica's meeting with Marshall and Mars's attack on her proved that Shaun's feelings for her had grown deeper than he'd realized.

She made him want to forget his guilt over his failure to prevent the deaths of his sister and the illegal immigrants at the border. He should have been smarter, faster, more aggressive. She made him want to unburden himself and let her comfort him, encourage him, heal him. She made him want to be whole and unwounded.

But he wasn't whole. He wouldn't be ever again. And he couldn't get close to a woman because it just wouldn't be fair to her. Eventually, he'd fail her. He'd fail to protect her, like he'd failed to protect so many people. And when that happened, the pain would be so deep and raw that he'd be nothing better than an animal.

Shaun checked the wireless internet router box and tightened a loose connection. Then he went back to the computer and saw his image in the screen. "Your video camera is set up."

"Thanks." Monica went to close the library door and crossed the room to sit at the desk.

Shaun positioned himself to the side of her, where he could see her computer screen but out of range of the video camera.

With a few clicks of the mouse, Monica connected to Lassiter's computer, and a tanned face appeared in the screen.

Shaun's dad hadn't grown up wealthy, but he'd made much of his money by the time Shaun was born, and so Shaun was familiar with some of the high-end clothing and accessories—including the sunglasses Lassiter wore, flashy and meant to announce to people that the wearer could afford to spend thousands of dollars just on a pair of shades. However, the shape of the glasses was wrong for his face. It made his face appear even more long and narrow than it already was. He also had a long nose without much of a bridge, so the glasses were already slipping down. Lassiter raised a hand to adjust his glasses, and the diamonds crusting his watch winked in the sunlight.

Shaun disliked the man on sight.

"Hi there, Monica."

"Hi, Rodney. Thank you for making time to talk to me today."

He gave a half smile. "I'm sitting next to the pool at the Efken Hotel right now, so it's not really a hardship."

Shaun grit his teeth at the way the man seemed to deliberately drop the name of the most exclusive, expensive hotel in

Miami. Unknown to most people, his father had done some consulting work for the owner several years ago.

At least Lassiter didn't waste time flirting with Monica the way Marshall had. His face was almost expressionless as he said, "Shall we get down to business? I'm afraid the only reason I'm at the pool bar is because I'm expecting to meet with one of our clients in about thirty minutes."

"Certainly. Did you get my invitation for the party?"

"Party?" Rodney's dark brows creased. "I'm afraid not. When did you send it? I've been in Florida for about two or three weeks now." From the looks of his tan, he seemed to be telling the truth, but how to know for certain?

Monica went on to explain about the party she was throwing for the investors in the clinic, and also to answer his questions about the project. Her face was cool and professional, but Shaun noticed that her eyes kept searching Rodney's face. What was she looking for?

As she talked, Shaun's mind churned. Something about this guy just didn't sit right with him. But a part of him realized it might simply be that he didn't like Lassiter very much.

He remembered his fleeting thought about Lassiter's tan, and his comment that he'd been in Florida for several weeks. He'd seemed to mention the hotel deliberately, but since this was an internet call, he could be anywhere—including out in someone's backyard in Sonoma. How to know that Lassiter really was in Florida?

And then he had an idea.

Shaun turned to where the Grants' wireless internet router sat on the bottom shelf of a bookcase, and he deliberately disconnected the internet.

"Rodney? Rodney?" Monica looked at Shaun and saw him squatting beside the router. "What are you doing?"

"Just making sure he's telling the truth." Shaun picked up Monica's cell phone where it sat on the desk, put it on speakerphone, and dialed his father's administrative assistant. "Hi, Lynn, it's Shaun. Could you please do me a favor? I was talking to a guy at the Efken Hotel in Miami and we got cut off, and I can't get him back on his cell phone. I know he's by the pool. Can you patch me into the manager at the Efken? Thanks."

Monica regarded him suspiciously. "How would your father know the manager at the Efken?"

"It's not common knowledge, but the Efken was struggling a few years ago. The owner called my father in to consult with them. Dad also asked me to consult with them on their security layout at the time." Shaun then turned his attention back to the cell phone as the Efken manager answered.

"Hello, Baker Worley speaking."

"Baker, it's Shaun O'Neill, Patrick O'Neill's son."

"Shaun! Nice to hear from you again."

"I was wondering if you could do me a favor. I was video chatting with Rodney Lassiter who's sitting beside the pool, and I lost my internet connection. I don't know his cell phone number, but could you patch me in to the bartender at the pool and ask him to give the phone to Rodney?"

"Oh, sure."

"So, has Rodney been giving you any problems?" Shaun asked in a jovial voice. "If he has, just tell me and I'll rough him up for you."

"Oh, of course not." Baker chuckled.

"How long has he been staying with you guys? Do you know?"

"Uh…over a week, at least. No, it's more like two or three weeks. He's got the Presidential Suite, and I had to turn away an actress and a country singer who both called and wanted to stay in the suite at the last minute, but Mr. Lassiter has it for another week or two."

"You should have sent them both up. Rodney would have

had a kick out of it." Shaun faked a laugh. "Sorry to take up your time, Baker. I'll let you get back to work. If you could please patch me through to Rodney?"

"Certainly, Shaun."

Baker put them on hold, then a minute later, a voice answered, "This is Danny at the Rowan Terrace bar. How can I help you?"

Monica said, "Danny, my name is Monica Grant. Could you please give the telephone to Rodney Lassiter? He should be sitting at the bar."

"Could you please wait a moment, Ms. Grant?"

"Yes."

There was a short, muffled conversation, then, "Hello?" Rodney Lassiter's nasally voice came on the line.

So Lassiter really was in Florida, and had apparently been there for a few weeks.

"Rodney, it's Monica Grant. I'm so sorry, but for some reason, my internet went down."

"I wondered what had happened. I tried calling your cell phone but was shunted to voice mail."

"I was probably calling the hotel to try to connect with you," Monica said.

"I'm afraid I need to meet with my client in a few minutes."

"Will you be at my party in a few days?"

Lassiter paused. "Could I ask you a question?"

"Of course."

"Could you... Do you..." This was the first time in the entire conversation that Lassiter seemed unsure and hesitant.

Monica's brow wrinkled as she looked at the phone sitting on the desk. "Yes?"

His question came out in a rush. "I hope I'm not being rude in asking this, but will Phillip Bromley be there?"

Shaun and Monica stared at each other in surprise. Then Monica recovered and replied, "Uh…why do you ask?"

"I don't mean to… I saw you talking to Phillip at the Zoe banquet a few minutes before you and I were introduced. Is he a close friend of yours?"

"He's…a potential investor. Is he a friend of yours?"

Lassiter didn't answer right away, and his uncharacteristic manner made Shaun lean closer to the phone.

Finally, he said, "Please keep this in confidence, because I don't wish to spread rumors about Phillip. I'm not even sure if what I saw was real. But I thought I saw him a few days ago."

"In Florida?"

"That's why at first I didn't think it was Phillip. His bank is in San Francisco."

"Where did you see him?"

"It was late. I'd met a client for dinner. The restaurant valet had brought my car around, but I was in the middle of a conversation with my client, so the valet left the car parked a few yards from the restaurant doors. By the time my client and I said goodbye, the valets had gone off to fetch some other cars. I went around to get into my car, but before I could even open the door, I heard an engine. It seemed louder than it should be, so I looked around and a car was gunning right for me.

"I jumped back out of the way. The car almost hit me. I looked at the driver and I thought it looked like Phillip Bromley. But I don't know why Phillip would want to hurt me."

Shaun didn't understand. Why would Phillip Bromley try to run down Rodney Lassiter? Had it really been Phillip? Lassiter was a potential investor. If Phillip was the stalker, would he harm the investors to force Monica to stop work on the clinic?

"When did this happen?" Monica asked.

"Four days ago."

The same day she'd had her first meeting with an investor. The stalker hadn't sent photos of Monica from that day. Maybe because he was in Miami trying to run down Rodney Lassiter?

"I'm…" Monica took a quick breath. "I'm sorry, I don't know if Mr. Bromley will be at the party."

"Even if he weren't attending, I'm not sure I'd be able to travel to Sonoma," Lassiter said. "I have a few more clients I need to meet with here in Florida, and I may not be done with my business by then. However, please do keep me updated on your project. I'm very interested in it."

As Monica disconnected her call with Lassiter, the sound of the doorbell reached them through the closed library door. "I wonder who that is? The mail already came this morning."

"Package delivery?" Shaun went to the library door and opened it. He was in time to see Evita open the front door and let in Detective Carter.

The detective strode into the foyer, his face grim, and caught sight of Shaun. "Is Monica with you, Shaun?"

"Yes."

"I need to speak to both of you."

"Come into the library." Shaun stood aside for him to enter, and then shut the door.

"I need you both to tell me what happened at Rock Love restaurant two days ago," the detective said.

"Rock Love?" Monica asked. "Did Brett file an incident report or something like that?"

The detective hesitated, his gray eyes moving from Monica to Shaun and back again. "Why didn't you tell me about it?"

Monica's gaze slid guiltily to Shaun's. "I didn't want to file charges."

"Did Mars file charges?" Shaun demanded.

"No," Detective Carter said. "What exactly did Mars do and say?"

"Detective, what's going on?" Monica said. "Are we in trouble?"

He hesitated again, but his granite expression softened as he looked at Monica, and a small sigh escaped him.

"Yesterday in Sonoma, Brett Marshall was mugged."

Five days after the last envelope of photos, a note finally arrived from the stalker.

If you do not stop work on your free children's clinic, I will harm all your investors. You do not want that on your conscience. I will do what I must in order to stop you.

Monica sat at her desk in her bedroom and watched Shaun read the note that had arrived that morning. As he read, his face became like a steel mask. He tossed the note onto her desk. "He doesn't directly say he's the one who mugged Marshall, but he implies it."

"And don't forget Rodney," Monica said.

"He said that it was Phillip Bromley."

"But he also said he wasn't sure."

She expected Shaun to argue with her, but he instead nodded. "Plus the car must have been going past him pretty fast and he wouldn't have gotten more than a quick look."

A part of her was a bit proud of Shaun for keeping his promise and keeping an open mind about the stalker, rather than being quick to pin it on Phillip.

"Did you talk to Marshall?" Shaun asked.

"He was discharged from the hospital this morning, so I called him at home. He said he's feeling fine, all things considered. He said he had gotten stitches for a gash on his forehead, his nose had been broken, he had several broken ribs, and he had a slight concussion, but he'd insisted on leaving the hospital rather than spending another minute there."

"Did the attacker steal anything?"

"No, he just beat Brett up pretty badly."

"Did Marshall see who did it?"

"He said he didn't see anything. And the police apparently have no evidence."

Shaun paced back and forth. "Are you going to cancel the party?"

"I have to." She dropped her head into her hands. The party was to have been in only a couple days, but she couldn't go through with it now.

Shaun sat in the chair across from her and leaned his arms on her desk. "How much is it costing you?"

"The deposit for the caterer and the event hall. A few thousand dollars." She winced.

"It's coming out of your own money?"

"Of course," she said, offended. "I wouldn't ask my father for a loan for this."

He raised his hands up. "I'm sorry, I didn't mean anything by it."

"No, I'm sorry for snapping at you. It's just…I'm losing so much more than this party. I had to call the investors this morning. I told them that I'd been getting anonymous threats from someone opposed to the clinic, and that one of the investors was attacked two days ago. Several of them automatically pulled out."

She'd spent so much time and energy into getting people to commit to this project, to make them aware of the need in Sonoma, and now her plans were unraveling. Was there more she could have done? What should she do to save it?

"Not all of them, though, right?" Shaun asked.

"I was surprised because some of them didn't seem to take the threats very seriously. One investor was annoyed because she'd already flown up here to northern California and was at the Rubart Hotel in Sonoma. She wanted me to go through with the party since she was already here."

Shaun snorted.

"Another investor said he was used to idle threats from strangers who objected to what he'd decided to invest in."

"I guess I can see how that wouldn't seem threatening anymore if it happened a few times," Shaun said, "but still, I don't understand that kind of thinking."

"It seems reckless, doesn't it? But then I called Brett Marshall, and the first thing he asked me was if I was going to cancel the party. He didn't want me to. He was urging me to go through with it because any large project that causes change will have protestors."

"Brett Marshall is used to taking risks. He's been very successful because of that. But he hasn't had a stalker like you do."

"I didn't tell the other investors about the stalker, but I told Brett. He still thought I should go through with the party. Apparently, he'd had opposition to several of his restaurants before they opened. He had received bomb threats, but for opening day, he just beefed up his security and had suspicious people escorted out. Nothing happened. And this was for each of the last three restaurants he opened."

Shaun grunted. "I didn't know about the bomb threats."

"Neither did I."

"So are you going to go through with the party?"

"Absolutely not. Brett spent a good twenty minutes trying to convince me."

Shaun looked thoughtful. "I have to admit, his opinion holds a lot of weight since he was the investor attacked because of your clinic. But I think you're wise to cancel the party."

She swallowed the bitter taste at the back of her throat. "I'm not sure what to do next. And what's even more frustrating is that after speaking to the six investors from the Zoe banquet who could be the stalker, I couldn't tell if any of them was lying to me."

Shaun looked at her strangely. "Did you really expect to?"

"I've always been good at reading people. I guess I've been depending on it too much all my life. Yes, I really did think I'd be able to tell if one of them was the stalker, but I couldn't read anything odd, uncomfortable, or threatening about any of them."

"What do you mean? Jason Mars tried to haul you out of the booth."

"He was angry about his wife and Brett, not the clinic. He didn't strike me as threatening at all when I spoke to him about the project. He only went berserk when I mentioned Brett Marshall."

The two of them sat in thoughtful silence for several minutes. Finally Monica said, "I'm starting to think that maybe the stalker isn't one of my investors at all."

"What do you mean? He knew about the party."

"Maybe he's close to one of my investors and found out about the invitation from that person."

Shaun sighed. "So he could be anyone. One of the investors' friends, family..."

"However, he definitely went to the Zoe banquet. Otherwise, why would I have smelled the cigarette scent in the cloakroom? But it doesn't mean I actually talked to the stalker about my clinic. He could have happened to overhear me talking to one of the twenty people I spoke to about it."

"We could call the event coordinator and get the guest list," Shaun said slowly. "But it'll be tedious to go through all the names, and there's no guarantee we'll find anything."

"It's worth a shot." Monica reached for her cell phone. "I can't think of anything else I can do now. I think I have Carol Uzaki's number."

But before she could pick up the phone, it rang. The Caller ID said it was Brett Marshall. "Hello."

"Monica, I have great news for you, but first you'll need

to give me the list of investors you were going to invite to your party."

"Why? Besides, several of them have already dropped out of the project."

"Then they'll be missing out."

Monica frowned, which made Shaun frown at her. "What do you mean?" she asked Brett.

"I'm not in any shape to go to a party in a few day's time—"

"Brett, I already canceled my party."

"I know, and I understand your position, but I don't like someone else trying to dictate to me how I spend my money, especially when there doesn't seem to be any good reason for why a free children's clinic shouldn't open in Sonoma."

"I told you, this stalker might have targeted another free clinic worker in L.A. Who knows what's going through his mind?"

"I understand why you had to cancel, but that doesn't mean I can't do something. So next week, *I'm* hosting a party for your investors at Rock Love restaurant."

TEN

As Shaun glanced around the banquet room, he felt the danger in the air like the shimmer of heat that rose from hot asphalt on a July day.

Twenty-three investors had agreed to attend the party despite being told about the anonymous threats Monica had been receiving. Apparently, Brett Marshall's attitude about protestors wasn't uncommon. Several of them had received letters of protest and criticism for various projects they'd invested in, although few of them had actually been threatened the way Marshall and Monica had. Of the six investors Monica had met at the Zoe banquet, only Marshall and Phillip Bromley had come tonight.

Shaun sidestepped a waiter, one of twelve who had been hand-selected by Marshall himself. They wore distinctive uniforms so Marshall could pick them out of the crowd and so he would notice if any of the wait staff was someone he didn't recognize.

Marshall had also hired several security guards to prevent strangers from entering the back room where the party was being held, and while the cooking staff was extra busy with both the regular restaurant patrons and the party, Marshall had refused to hire new staff that he or his chefs wouldn't recognize.

Shaun had to admit that the man had given this party a great deal of forethought. Shaun and Monica had offered suggestions for improving security, but most of the ideas had come from the restaurant owner himself.

Still, Shaun couldn't shake the way his skin crawled as he surveyed the room. It had been a business casual event, but most of the men wore expensive Italian suits, and the women were in deceptively simple short dresses that probably cost his entire year's salary.

He'd grown up in this world of wealth, but he'd gladly left it behind to join the border patrol. He'd become just Shaun O'Neill there, not the son of a hotel mogul.

However, Monica moved through this world with ease. Not that she was snobby or that she flaunted her father's wealth, but she wore her finery with the comfort of a woman who had attended many parties with her father and sisters, or sometimes in her father's place when he had had his stroke. She walked with grace and elegance as she approached an investment banker to speak to him.

Shaun was here for her—not to fit in with these people, not to be her right-hand business partner, not to work the party. That's all she wanted from him, and she trusted him completely.

So he better earn her trust.

He'd memorized the faces of the waitstaff, and as he scanned the people mingling together and the few tables along the walls, he didn't see anyone who shouldn't be there. He'd gone with Marshall's security guards to check each of the tables and make sure there hadn't been any mysterious packages left, but the guards knew what they were doing, since they'd had to do a similar drill for each of Marshall's three restaurants that had received bomb threats.

He had matched each of the guests to the guest list as they entered, but he was beginning to wonder, like Monica did, if the stalker wasn't an investor, but someone connected to an investor who had been invited. In fact, maybe it had been an investor who pulled out last week after Marshall was mugged, and so the stalker didn't even know about this party.

The sense he had of a threat didn't go away as the evening progressed. When the salads started being served, he slipped away to the kitchen.

He watched the cooking staff like a hawk. He also watched the main courses be plated, but nothing seemed unusual.

He approached Marshall's chef, Tracy, who had been put in charge of the party menu. "What's for dessert?" Shaun asked her.

"Why, want to sneak a taste?" She paused to wink at him, then continued wiping the edge of a plate and sending it out with a waiter. "Since you're one of the guests, I suppose you can eat yours early. They're chocolate macadamia nut mousses in the fridge."

He entered the massive walk-in refrigerator and quickly found the two trays of mousses sitting on shelves, one on top of the other. Dark chocolate mousse, dotted with macadamia nuts, had been swirled into decorative glass bowls, with a stick of white chocolate stuck into each mousse at an angle.

But as he surveyed them all, he noticed something odd.

In between several mousse bowls were clear droplets of water on the stainless steel tray. There wasn't anything on the shelf above the top tray of desserts, so the water hadn't dripped onto the tray from something else. But also, the water drops were on both trays, not just the top one. And mousses weren't clear, so it couldn't have come from the desserts themselves.

Shaun stepped out of the refrigerator and glanced around. The rest of the cooking staff raced around to serve the restaurant guests and didn't pay any attention to him. And then he noticed that the back door to the restaurant lay only a few yards to his right. The produce was delivered every day and it wouldn't make sense to have to carry it more than a few feet from the delivery door.

But it also meant someone could walk into the kitchen, then into the refrigerator, and then leave without being noticed.

Maybe he was being paranoid. Maybe it was only water. How would the stalker know that those mousses were for the party?

He went back to Tracy. "I need to talk to you."

"Can it wait?"

"No."

She sighed and turned to him. "What is it?"

"When did you make the mousses?"

She looked up as she thought. "Around two this afternoon."

"Were the trays wet when you put the mousses on them?"

"Wet?" She blinked at him. "No, they hadn't been used. I got them out of the storage cabinet."

He led her into the fridge and pointed out the water. She looked up at the empty rack above the desserts, and also at the ceiling of the refrigerator. "Maybe condensation from the ceiling...?"

"But it's on both trays. It would make sense if the water was only on the top tray, but it's on the bottom tray of desserts, too."

Tracy's lips narrowed as she surveyed the water drops. "Brett told me about the threat to the investors, but do you really think...?"

"I don't know. When I was working for the border patrol, I tasted cyanide and arsenic. Cyanide was bitter and acidic, but arsenic dissolved in water didn't taste like anything. It was just like water."

Like the drops on the trays.

"So you think someone came in and dosed all these mousses with arsenic?" Tracy asked.

"Or something. They could have used a dropper, and if they were working fast, some of the poison would have dropped between the bowls."

"But I've been in the kitchen all afternoon. I didn't notice anyone coming in here to tamper with the desserts."

"The kitchen's been busy because of the party. Would you have noticed if someone snuck in from the back door? It would only take a second or two to get from the door to the refrigerator."

Tracy shook her head, but she heaved a frustrated sigh. "Then what do I serve for dessert?"

Shaun didn't have an answer for her.

"Never mind," Tracy said. "I'll think of something. Let's throw these away first."

"No, we have to keep them, but maybe we can put them away someplace where no one will eat them. I'll find a way to get them tested to see if they really were poisoned."

"I suppose it's better to be safe than sorry." Tracy grabbed one of the trays and led the way out of the fridge. "I was here when they were checking for bombs the day the restaurant opened. There are some crazy people out there."

Shaun followed her, carrying the other tray. "Where should we put these?"

"Nowhere in this kitchen. You don't want anyone accidentally sneaking a bite. Can you put them in your car?"

They laid the trays in the back of his Suburban, then returned to the restaurant.

"You need to tell them dessert will be delayed," Tracy said. "I've got to come up with something."

Shaun entered the banquet room and approached the podium at the front. Monica had everything set up for the presentation she was going to give later in the evening, including a microphone that fed into speakers placed along the top of the walls.

Shaun turned the mike on and cleared his throat. "Excuse me, folks."

The room hushed, and Monica turned to look at him with wide eyes. He tried to smile to assure her, but it only made her look more frightened.

"The chef asked me to tell you that dessert will be delayed a bit," Shaun said. "I know most of you are almost done with your meals, so maybe Monica can begin her presentation a bit early?"

Several guests clapped as Monica rose and approached the podium, her smile fixed on her face.

"I'll explain later," he murmured to her before walking back into the sea of tables. He positioned himself near the back of the room, standing against the wall.

As she began her presentation, Shaun wasn't surprised when Marshall left his seat to stand next to him. "What happened?" he asked in a hard voice.

"I think the dessert was poisoned."

"Impossible. I didn't hire any temporary help for the kitchen staff."

"It would still have been easy for someone to get into the fridge from the back door and dose the desserts. No one would have seen them."

Marshall stood tall and rigid next to Shaun, his eyes on Monica. "Where are they?"

"In my car. I'll have them tested."

"You better be right. I don't like being told someone is messing with my restaurant." He left Shaun to sit back down.

Messing with his restaurant was the least of his worries. If they'd eaten the desserts, within thirty minutes, they might all have been dead.

* * *

That night, after dropping Monica off at her home, Shaun was so exhausted that when the automatic garage door lifted only twelve inches before grinding to a halt, he didn't even notice that the outdoor floodlights hadn't turned on until he'd already climbed out of the truck.

He paused, standing next to the SUV's open door, squinting at the dark floodlights that should have illuminated the entire front driveway of his father's home. The only light was from his headlights, which reflected off the mostly closed garage door, and the lights from the inside of the garage, which shone under the bottom edge.

And then out of the corner of his eye, he saw a shadow move.

Remembering the shovel outside of Monica's home, he ducked.

Clang! Something metallic hit the frame of his truck above his head. He didn't stop to look—he tackled the dark figure, and they flew through the air before landing hard on the gravel driveway.

Bits of gravel rained against his face, both from the impact and because the figure quickly scrambled to get away from him. Blows rained sharply on Shaun's head and shoulders, and he struggled to pin the man down.

The two men twisted wildly, Shaun trying to wrestle the man into a jiujitsu submission. He pulled the man's head down to do a guillotine choke, but the attacker began punching at Shaun's ribs near the place where a bullet had grazed him last year. The pain made stars flash in front of his eyes, and he loosened his hold.

The attacker began to slither away from him, but Shaun used his legs around the stalker's waist to hold him fast while he also clenched hard on the man's head, grabbing fistfuls of hair. The man's harsh, fast breathing sounded loud in the still night air.

The attacker was tiring.

Then with one swift move, the man yanked himself away. Shaun pulled a hank of hair loose as the man shot backward. He flipped in midair to land on his hands and knees, and then took off into the darkness.

Shaun started to jump to his feet, but a sudden sharp pain in his side made him stumble. His old injury. He grit his teeth and pelted after the man, but each step felt like a knife stabbed him in the ribs.

He was still yards away when he saw headlights blaze to life, and then a car take off down the road from his house. Shaun hadn't even seen the car when he'd pulled into his driveway. His father's home was like the Grants' house, widely spaced between neighbors on ten acres of land with lots of bushes and trees for a car to hide behind.

His lungs burned, and his side was on fire. Muscles he hadn't used in months ached all through his arms and legs. But as he glanced down at his hands, he realized he wasn't completely empty-handed.

He still had the hair he'd pulled from the attacker's head.

Monica's nerves were walking on a knife blade. The stalker hadn't done anything in over a week.

Something terrible was due at any time, and soon.

She parked in the O'Neills' driveway, and after getting the first-aid kit out of her car, she headed toward the front door, but before she could ring, Shaun opened it for her.

"Come on in." He stepped aside for her. "I don't want you outside and exposed for too long."

Still watching out for her, even though his old torso injury had kept him in bed for several days after the attack. "How's your side feeling?"

"Better every day."

"Let me look at it."

He led her into the living room, where every flat surface had accumulated old sports pages from the newspaper, empty and half-empty drinking cups and mugs, and plates covered with crumbs. "Sorry for the mess. Dad still hasn't hired a housekeeper yet, even though he opened the house up again a month ago."

In fact, a couple of chairs still had Holland covers thrown over them, while others had only had the covers folded aside but still half-hanging off the backs. When she'd visited him other times this past week, she'd only seen his bedroom since he'd been unable to move without pain. His room was immaculate, but she hadn't realized until now that the rest of the house was still in a state of disarray.

She rested the first-aid kit on top of a stack of newspapers on the coffee table while Shaun gingerly sat down on the couch.

"Any letters or photos from our friend?" Shaun pulled up one side of his shirt to expose his wound.

"Nothing." Monica gently removed the tape adhering the sterile gauze square to his side.

"It makes me wonder what he's up to."

"Me, too." The attacker's blows had reopened the wound a little, but by now the flesh was starting to heal. "I also don't know why he's not claiming responsibility for the attack on you."

"I was thinking about it last night," Shaun said. "I think he attacked me because I stopped the poisoning at the party. He might have been angry at me, or he might have wanted to get me out of the way to leave you more vulnerable."

Monica paused as she soaked a cotton ball with antiseptic solution. She had come to depend on Shaun being there for her. What would she do if he'd been more seriously hurt?

She didn't want to think about it. "Rachel called me this morning to say that she got the lab results back."

Monica's dermatologist sister Rachel had explained that since the Sonoma PD was so small, they used a freelance laboratory to do their forensic work, and their workload was typically large. To get results faster, Rachel had sent the hair Shaun had grabbed as well as the poisoned mousses to a different freelance laboratory she often used for chemical analysis of her skin care products.

"And?" Shaun winced as Monica dabbed antiseptic on his wound.

"You were right. The mousses were poisoned with arsenic." The news had sent a shock through her when Rachel had told her.

Shaun, too, stilled. "It's the kind of thing you don't really want to hear."

"But Rachel also said that it hadn't been a lethal concentration. People would have gotten sick, but they wouldn't necessarily have died. He might have made a mistake in the amount of arsenic." She tore open a package of sterile gauze.

"What about the hair?"

"It's actually blond, dyed brown."

He stared at the dark television on the far wall of the living room as he thought. "Phillip's hair used to be blond when he was a teenager. It might have gotten darker with age, or he might dye it."

Monica attached the gauze over his wound with medical tape. "I'm not sure that most men—who don't have gray hair—will bother to dye their hair a normal color. Funky colors, sometimes. But to dye it brown? Why?"

"To disguise himself." Then he reluctantly conceded, "Which wouldn't make sense in Phillip's case."

"Rachel also had the lab analyze the DNA, and the lab's checking the various databases, but nothing yet. It could be

that the attacker's DNA isn't in the system. There, I'm done."
She smoothed the last piece of tape against his skin, and felt
his muscles move beneath her fingers.

While dressing his wound, she'd been able to go into nursing mode and simply focus on the task, not the man. But now
she became uncomfortably aware of his scent, and his nearness, and the silkiness of his skin under her hand.

She forced her hands into her lap.

Shaun dropped his shirt down over the bandage again. "I
got a call from Nathan a few minutes before you got here. He
heard back from his friends in the LAPD."

"Did they look into Clare's death again?"

"Not exactly. At the time, they hadn't had the information
about the stalker targeting women working for free clinics,
but Nathan had them search the database for other suicides.
He found two of them in the years since Clare's death."

She leaned forward. "Two? Who were they?"

"One was a girl who worked for another free family planning clinic. The other worked for a free urgent care facility.
But their deaths were different from Clare's."

"Not drug overdoses?"

"No. One hung herself, the other took sleeping pills and
alcohol."

Those poor women. Monica looked down at her hands.
"So, no other connection to Clare's death?"

"Actually, because the deaths had been suicides, the police
hadn't investigated further. But when they found the free
clinic association, they looked to see if the girls had filed incident reports about a stalker. And both of them had."

"What?" Monica's spine stiffened.

"Both women had lived alone. It could be that they hadn't
told many of their friends or family members about the
stalker, so no one connected the stalker with their suicides.

Or maybe they just didn't question it aggressively when the police ruled their deaths suicides."

She took a few deep breaths to calm herself. "So this guy could have been continuing to stalk women in L.A. for all these years. And then killing them if they didn't stop work on their free clinics, but making them look like suicides."

"It's not just coincidence anymore," Shaun said. "It's a pattern."

She rose to her feet and walked to the large bay window, looking out into the trees in front of the house. "I thought that if I ever had confirmation that this stalker and Clare's stalker were the same—if I had proof as opposed to just co-incidence, that I'd feel better. But I don't feel better. I just feel more afraid."

Shaun got up and stood behind her, putting his hand on her shoulder. "Don't be afraid. I'm here for you."

She touched his hand briefly, savoring this moment being close to him, then made herself move away. "I suppose…I guess this means we have more information about him, so we're more likely to find him, right?" She tried to force herself to be determined, to be positive. Otherwise, she would be tempted to give in to the fear.

She supposed that meant they had more information on him, so they were more likely to find him. She tried to force herself to be determined, to be positive. Otherwise, she would be tempted to give in to the fear.

She also had news Shaun wasn't going to like. "I got a call from Phillip Bromley today."

His mouth tightened.

"He wants to meet me for lunch tomorrow at a café near his bank in San Francisco. He has a friend who may be interested in investing in the clinic."

Shaun gave her an incredulous look. "Does this friend know about everything that happened?"

"Phillip said he told him everything, and he's still interested."

Shaun shook his head violently and began pacing in front of the large flat-screen television. "No, this is too suspicious. It's a trap."

"In a café in broad daylight? At lunch hour in San Francisco?"

"After what happened at the party, I'm not letting you near that murderer," he spat out.

His ferocity made her flinch. "Shaun…"

"He's trying to get you alone so he can do something worse—"

"I told Phillip that if I decided to meet him, I'd be bringing you."

Shaun paused his pacing, but then resumed it with renewed anger. "Maybe he's being cocky."

"You promised me—"

"I know he's the stalker," Shaun said with a raised voice.

She paused before saying, "Shaun, this is…this is starting to be vindictive."

He gave her a look she couldn't interpret, then turned to stare out the window. She watched him carefully and saw his stiff shoulders relax bit by bit.

Finally he turned back to her. "He knows I'll be with you?"

"In fact, he seemed fine with that."

"In broad daylight. In a busy restaurant."

"So do I have my bodyguard's permission to have lunch with Phillip tomorrow?"

He gave a curt nod.

At that moment, her cell phone rang. The caller ID showed it was Carol Uzaki, the founder of Zoe International and the hostess of the "thank you" dinner for Zoe's sponsors a few weeks ago. "Hi, Carol."

Carol answered with her usual good cheer and enthusiastic friendliness. "Hi, Monica, how are you doing? It was so good to see you at the Zoe banquet. I'm so sorry your dad couldn't come, but it was wonderful to catch up with you and your sisters."

"Thanks, Carol. I wish we'd had more time to chat."

"Me, too! We're heading back to Thailand tomorrow. Anyway, I emailed you that guest list you wanted. I hope it helps you. I'll be praying for you."

Monica didn't know how to respond. She hadn't told Carol about the stalker. "Thanks, Carol."

"And remember that Jesus is always in control, whether things are going good, or bad, or great, or downhill. Oh, Monica." And Monica could hear the smile in Carol's voice. "You are so precious to Jesus. You matter so deeply to Him. Don't ever forget that, okay?"

The words made tears sting her eyes. She turned away so Shaun couldn't see. "Okay."

"I've got to go. So much to do before we go back. Bye!"

She stood there a moment, the phone to her ear, her brain and her heart trying to understand the strange and strangely wonderful things Carol had said to her. They had moved her in a way she hadn't felt before, which she couldn't quite explain.

She'd think about all this later, when the stress of the moment wasn't overwhelming her.

She turned to Shaun. "Carol emailed me the guest list. Did you want to take a quick look before we go talk to Phillip?"

He searched her face for a moment, his eyes worried, but then he nodded and led the way to his father's office across the hallway. She hopped on to the internet and logged into her email account, then opened Carol's message and the attachment.

The guest list was actually an extensive spreadsheet that gave information about each guest. Carol had erased guests' addresses and phone numbers, but all the other information was there, including table assignments, number of people in their party, and then a column on the far right that indicated whether the ticket had been given to the guest or if they had bought the ticket.

"What's that column for?" Shaun asked, puzzled. "I thought all the guests at the Zoe banquet were donors to Zoe International, and that's why they were given tickets. I didn't realize people could buy tickets."

"It's for if the guest wants to bring other people," Monica said. "Dad donates to Zoe, so he gets two tickets—one for him and one for Aunt Becca. Naomi, Rachel and I also donate to Zoe, but nowhere near as much money as Dad, so we aren't automatically given tickets. This year, he didn't go, so Aunt Becca and I went on the two free tickets, and we bought tickets for Naomi and Rachel."

She scrolled through the list, looking for names of people she'd talked to. One of the first she saw was Phillip's name, and then she realized something very strange.

Monica pointed to the screen. "Look at this. He isn't a donor to Zoe, he bought his ticket on his own."

"So?"

She scrolled down quickly to look at everyone else who'd bought a ticket. There weren't many, but they made it more obvious something was wrong. "These records indicate he was alone, he wasn't with any other party of people already invited. Everyone else bought a ticket in order to be included with some other party, like my family did. He's the *only* one who bought a ticket just to attend the banquet by himself."

Shaun frowned at the computer screen. "The only one? Out of, what, three hundred guests?"

Monica stared at Phillip's name on the spreadsheet. She really hadn't thought he had anything underhanded in mind whenever she spoke to him, but this caused a tremble of unease in her chest.

If Phillip wasn't a donor to Zoe International, why in the world had he gone to the Zoe banquet?

As soon as Shaun saw Phillip Bromley's face, a surge of anger rolled in his gut.

Shaun had been trying to be open-minded and not jump to conclusions, but he knew the man was hiding something. Eventually evidence would begin to point to Phillip as being responsible for his sister's death, and for the threats against Monica.

And Shaun wasn't going to let him get away with it.

As Phillip rose from a table at the café near his San Francisco bank, he darted a glance at Shaun, but then ignored him and greeted Monica with a smile. "Hi, Monica. This is Dr. Harold Uzaki. He's a pediatrician."

She shook hands with the smiling Japanese man. "Pleased to meet you." Monica sat at the table next to him. "This is my business associate, Shaun O'Neill," she said as Shaun pulled out a chair and lowered himself down.

"Thank you for making the time to meet with us," Dr. Uzaki said.

Phillip's polite smile slipped as he glanced again at Shaun, but then he nodded. "Shaun. Good to see you."

Shaun couldn't say the same, and he couldn't stop glaring at the man.

Phillip swallowed.

Monica noticed Shaun's black expression and shot him a look that was part concern and part command: *What's wrong? Calm down.* She turned to Harold Uzaki. "Are you related to Carol Uzaki from Zoe International?"

Harold's smile grew brighter. "Her husband is my cousin. In fact, my wife and I are both doctors and often visit their orphanage in Thailand to do free health check-ups on the children. That is why we're interested in your clinic, despite the attacks on it. We believe strongly in free medical care for children, no matter where they live."

As Harold and Monica chatted, Shaun tried to relax, but the politeness of the conversation grated on him. He wanted to grab Phillip by the collar and demand he tell them if he had killed Clare. That was a little harder to do with drinks and food on the table between them. It upset him that it was almost as if she were protecting Phillip when he could be the stalker.

Shaun was almost finished with the ham sandwich he'd ordered when a buzzing in his pocket made him look at his cell phone. It was Nathan.

He considered ignoring it, but the lunch situation seemed safe enough, so he excused himself, saying, "I'm sorry, I need to take this." He answered the phone as he walked a few paces away, keeping the table within his field of view and also within easy reach, but out of earshot if he kept his voice low. "Hey, Nathan."

"Shaun, I found something you'll be interested in."

Anticipation quickened in his gut. "Spill."

"I got my friend down in the Los Angeles Police Department to look up incident reports from Clare's neighborhood around the time she died that night. A woman two doors down from your sister's town house had called the police about an hour before Clare's estimated time of death. She reported a man with a long black coat hanging around her house.

"They also found out that a convenience-store clerk about a block away called the police because some kids were causing problems—making a mess, harassing the clerk. By the time the police got there, the kids were gone, but the clerk mentioned that a customer had tried to help the clerk get rid of the kids. A man had grabbed a kid and hauled him out of the store. The man hadn't stuck around, so he wasn't there when the police arrived, but the clerk mentioned that he was a 'friendly guy wearing a *Dresden Files* coat.'"

"Dresden Files?" The name sounded familiar—A TV show? A movie?

"It was a television show, and the main character wore a short black leather jacket."

"Not a duster?"

"Well, here's the interesting part. Because Clare's neighbor had mentioned a long coat, and because he knew about Phillip's duster coat, my LAPD friend looked up *Dresden Files* on the internet, and he found that there was both a television show and a book series. In the show, the character wore a black leather jacket, but in the books, he wears *a black leather duster.*"

The air was sucked out of his lungs, and he gasped for breath for a moment. "A duster, not just a long black coat?"

Nathan's voice became cautious. "Shaun, it doesn't point directly at Phillip. The information is only circumstantial."

"Nathan, he's the only one of Clare's friends to wear one."

"Look, my LAPD friend is going to try to find the clerk and show him a picture of Phillip—"

"The police never asked Phillip if he had an alibi for that night." Bitterness had crept into Shaun's voice. "There hasn't been anything to indicate he might have been near her house." Until now. He cast a look at Phillip's relaxed face, and his fists bunched.

"Shaun—"

"Thanks, Nathan." He disconnected the call and strode toward the table with a quick step. "Phillip, we need to talk," he demanded.

Monica's mouth opened in shock. "Shaun."

Phillip gaped at him like a fish out of water.

Dr. Uzaki, however, recovered more quickly than Monica or Phillip, and smiled politely as he stood. "It is obvious something important has occurred. Miss Grant, you have given me enough information about your clinic for me to be able to speak to my wife. I will call her now, if you'll excuse me." He walked toward the front of the café while pulling out his cell phone.

Shaun refused to sit down again, and he hovered over Phillip's nervous form. "Where were you the night my sister died?"

A tremor went through Phillip at the mention of Clare, and his eyes widened, but his face was otherwise still. "Clare? Why do you ask about Clare? That seems kind of odd." His hand reached up to cup his chin, with a finger covering the edge of his mouth.

Phillip was hiding something, and Shaun didn't know what, didn't know how to make him talk.

Monica seemed to pull herself together and took the situation in hand, probably to keep Shaun from embarrassing her further. She tugged on Shaun's wrist and forced him to take a seat.

Then she turned to Phillip. "You were friends with Clare, weren't you?" she asked in a gentle tone. But her eyes were steady on Phillip's face, and Shaun knew she was looking for any nuance, trying to read him.

"We hung out with the same crowd of people every so often. I'd see her at the same parties I went to, or some of the same nightclubs."

Nightclubs? It reminded Shaun of something Clare's roommate had said. "The night before Clare was found dead, she'd gone to a nightclub called The Chip. Were you there, too?"

Phillip's lips paled. "No. No, I've never gone there."

Monica's eyes narrowed. "I met the owner of The Chip a few months ago at a charity ball down in L.A. He said that

The Chip is unique because it has microchips that have a person's information, like a credit card number. The chips can be put in a piece of jewelry. The bartender and the door bouncers have scanners they use to read the microchips so people can enter and buy drinks without needing to bring their IDs." She leaned forward. "How about I call the owner and ask him if he'd look for your name in his records of chip holders?"

The owner of the nightclub would never do that, but Phillip obviously hadn't thought of that. He swallowed hard. "Oh, that place. I may have been there once or twice."

"So were you there the night Clare was?" Shaun asked.

"Uh…" His gaze moved to follow a waitress who happened to be walking between them and the table next to them. "I don't really remember."

Shaun felt his teeth grind against each other. "Tell me the truth, you lying little snake."

"I'm not lying. I was…I was…" Phillip's lips opened and closed, but no sound came out.

Shaun snapped at him. "Stop trying to make something up."

"I wasn't there," Phillip said in a high, tight voice.

"People saw a man who looked exactly like you, wearing a black leather duster," Shaun shouted. He dimly registered that the sounds of conversation around them quieted at his words.

"A…a black duster? There's…there's got to be a mistake." Phillip's face looked like the white flesh of a hard-boiled egg.

"Just admit it. You were there at my sister's apartment," Shaun persisted.

Phillip flinched. "It wasn't me," he cried. "It was…"

Silence fell between them. Phillip was breathing hard, his mouth tight and his eyes screwed shut. He pressed the flats of his palms against his forehead. "He's trying to set me up," he moaned.

Shaun could only stare at him, the anger pitching in his stomach. "Who's trying to set you up?"

"I don't know…some guy."

"Set you up for what?" Monica said.

Phillip rubbed his thumb into his palm and sat hunched at the table, his eyes on his lap. Finally, as if each word pained him, he said, "I know Clare didn't kill herself. She was murdered."

ELEVEN

The words hung in the air between them, and Shaun began to shake. His gut boiled and frothed. "You killed her."

"No!" Phillip's eyes were wild. "He tried to set me up."

"Who?" Monica said.

"I don't know who. I know…" A moan gusted out of him. "I gave Clare a ride home from The Chip that night. All I did was stop in front of her townhouse, walk her to the door, and then get back in my car to drive away. I drove maybe a block," Phillip said. "Then I realized I'd forgotten to ask her something. I don't even remember what, now. I stopped, and rather than making a three-point turn, I looked in the rear-view mirror to see if I could just back the car down the road to her townhouse. But I saw a guy…" His mouth pulled back, as if he was in pain. "I saw a guy in a black leather duster, just like mine, just like the one I'd been wearing that night. He crossed the street to Clare's townhouse, rang the doorbell, and she opened the door for him."

"You're saying Clare let another man into her townhouse that night?" Monica's mouth was open in surprise.

"And he happened to be wearing the same type of leather coat as you," Shaun sneered. "Nice story, Bromley."

"You've got to believe me, it's true," he said.

"Why didn't you tell anyone?" Monica asked.

"Tell someone? After Clare was found dead the next morning? Are you crazy? If I went forward and cast doubt that it hadn't been suicide, the police would investigate and all the evidence was going to point to *me,* not to some other guy who happens to wear the same eccentric coat as me. I was seen wearing that coat in all the same clubs that Clare went to."

Phillip covered his face with his hands, and his voice was muffled as he said, "No one else came forward to say they'd seen a guy in a duster being let into Clare's house that night. I knew I was the only one who'd seen him. I stayed quiet because any of the evidence would have gotten me in trouble."

"What evidence?" Monica said.

"Her roommate told me she had overdosed on heroin." Phillip's hands fell from his face. "I used heroin five years ago."

"And you still say you didn't kill her?" Shaun said. "You're sitting there and telling me you didn't stalk her and kill her?"

"Stalk her?" Phillip's mouth dropped open. "*Stalk her?* What are you talking about?"

Monica reached out a hand and touched his forearm. "You didn't know about the stalker?"

"She had a stalker?" Phillip fell back against his seat. "Oh, my goodness. That explains it."

"Explains what?" Monica said.

Phillip turned to her. "I swear, until this moment, I didn't know Clare had had a stalker. But whenever I hung out with her and her boyfriend wasn't around, she always seemed on edge. I even asked her about it, and she told me she was just stressed about work."

"How could you not know about the stalker?" Monica asked. "She confronted you about the snake venom."

"But she didn't say it was from a stalker. I thought it might have been from someone threatening her about the family planning clinic. Her boyfriend got threats and nasty gifts all the time."

Phillip then suddenly sat up straight, regarding Monica with understanding dawning in his eyes. "Clare's clinic. And *your* clinic. That's why you're asking me about Clare. *He's stalking you, too.*"

Phillip's entire face seemed to lengthen as he stared at her with wide eyes and wide mouth.

For a moment, Shaun believed his surprise. But then that same familiar feeling of helplessness washed over him, making him feel like he was drowning. Phillip couldn't be innocent. He had to be lying. He had to be Clare's killer. Shaun *had* to have finally found Clare's killer.

"I'm not stalking you, Monica," Phillip said, his words coming out fast and babbling. "I'm not. I promise. I know I've wanted to talk to you and get close to you, but it's not what it looks like. I swear."

"Why were you at the Zoe banquet?" Monica asked. "You deliberately bought a ticket."

Phillip's eyes darted to Shaun, then back to Monica. Then his eyes and mouth drooped as he said in a small voice, "I wanted to speak to Patrick O'Neill."

"My father? He and your dad don't even get along. Why would you want to talk to him?"

"I know, that's why I went to the Zoe banquet. I knew he'd be there. I want to partner with him in one of his hotels."

"What?" Shaun said. "You're a banker."

"With your dad's track record with hotels, it's sure to be a good investment. I've always wanted to go in on a hotel with him. That's one of the reasons I started hanging out with Clare all those years ago, to try to get close to him. But then Clare and I became real friends and I wasn't interested in her only to get to her father."

Shaun didn't realize his hands were in fists until he looked down and saw his white knuckles. He forced them to open but he couldn't get them to relax.

Phillip turned to Monica. "I went to the Zoe banquet and overheard Patrick talking to you about your dad's hotel. I didn't even know your father was Patrick's next hotel project until that moment. That's why I went to talk to you, and talk about the clinic, and maybe try to get involved in the new hotel."

Monica had stretched her shoulders and eased back in her seat, away from Phillip.

"I'm sorry," he said. "It's just that it's been something I've wanted for a long time, to work with Patrick O'Neill on one of his hotels. I don't want to be a VP at my dad's bank for the rest of my life."

She regarded him for a long time, her eyes assessing and observant. Then she pushed back her half-eaten sandwich. "I hope you don't mind, but I'm not hungry anymore. I think it's best we cut this lunch short. Please give our excuses to Dr. Uzaki when he returns."

"I'm still interested in your clinic," Phillip said earnestly.

Sure, he was. Shaun knew what Phillip was thinking. If he contributed to her clinic, she might still enable him to invest in her father's hotel. He didn't know that Augustus Grant would never allow an outside investor.

Monica's face was carefully neutral as she replied, "Thank you, Phillip. I'll contact you later about it." She stood up.

Shaun got to his feet and found that his entire body was trembling. He clenched his hands and walked out of the restaurant after Monica, but a part of his mind was shouting at him not to leave Phillip Bromley sitting there not paying for the consequences of his actions.

They had parked at the Union Square parking garage, but instead of steering them back to their car, Monica pulled

Shaun up the concrete steps to the park in the middle of Union Square. "Let's walk and clear our heads first."

He didn't need to clear his head. He knew what he needed to do. He needed to either prove Phillip Bromley was lying or find Clare's killer.

But Monica threaded her arm through his and pulled him along. They walked in silence for several minutes, passing other people in the park, circling the monument in the center of it. Monica looked up at the figure of a woman at the top of the tall column, called "Victory."

He didn't feel very victorious. He felt tied down. He was so close and yet nowhere nearer to finding out who killed Clare.

Finally Monica said, "Why are you so angry at him?"

"Because he's lying," Shaun snapped.

She stopped and turned to face him. "You remind me of Jason Mars."

"What? I'm nothing like Jason Mars."

"Do you remember when I told you about the first time I talked to him? I thought he had some kind of anger simmering under the surface, but I knew it had nothing to do with me or what we were talking about. We found out later he was angry because he thought Brett Marshall had seduced his wife."

Shaun didn't like where this conversation was going. "For all we know, Brett Marshall *did* seduce his wife."

Monica wasn't to be distracted. "Well, you're angry, too. And while you think you're angry at Phillip Bromley, you're really angry at *yourself.*"

Her words were like a punch to the gut, making the air whoosh out of his lungs. He stared at her for a moment, then pulled his arm away from her and started walking away.

She ran after him, tugged at his arm, made him stop. Then

she put her hands on either side of his face and made him look at her.

Her eyes were clear and soothing, like looking into a cup of tea. He couldn't speak, but her eyes seemed to be trying to read his thoughts so he wouldn't have to.

"Why are you angry at yourself?" she asked softly. "Is it because of Clare? You couldn't have done anything. It wasn't your fault."

"I could have been here," he mumbled. "I could have noticed something was wrong, I could have made her tell me about the stalker. I could have prevented her from moving to L.A."

"Oh, Shaun," she breathed. Her fingers caressed his face. "Hindsight is twenty-twenty. Do you really think you need to be a superhero?"

Maybe he did. He had so many people he had to take care of, not just Clare, but also the people at the border.... He looked away from her, but her hands were strong, and she forced his eyes back on hers.

"It's not just Clare," she said.

"Everyone I should protect dies," he blurted.

His words made her eyes widen, and she went rigid for a second. But then suddenly she pulled his head down and kissed him.

Her lips were warm and soft. It was as if she wanted to give him something he needed, something he lacked. As if she could give him the strength he needed.

He pulled back and they stared at each other for a long moment. Then she dropped her hands from his face, leaving his skin feeling cold.

She took his arm and led him to the steps leading up to the park, and then pulled him down to sit. "Why did you say that?" she asked him.

"Never mind."

"Tell me."

He didn't answer.

He shivered in a chill wind blowing in from the San Francisco Bay, making the city colder than the warm rolling hills of Sonoma or the hot beaches of southern California. She was trying to dig into a deeper part of him that he didn't want to uncover, a dark place he didn't want to go.

She searched his face with those clear eyes. "Something happened more recently than Clare's death. Something that's still raw and hurts you."

Images rose up in his mind. He'd joined the border patrol to right wrongs, but it seemed there were more and more wrongs committed every day that he couldn't fix. The coyotes, the men who smuggled Mexican nationals over the border into America, were ruthless and completely without morals. Time and again, he'd see the coyotes commit horrible atrocities to their human charges and get away with it.

The last straw had been a car chase that ended with the coyote driving a van of people over the edge of an embankment and into a raging river. The coyote had swum to safety, but the people had been locked in the van. Shaun had plunged into the water to try to get to the van before it sank, but he'd had to watch as the people drowned in front of him—men, women, children. He heard their fists pounding against the metal sides of the van as it sank below the waters, as he tried to swim faster and get to them. He dove to try to find the van, to open a door before it sank too far, but he couldn't dive deep enough.

"They all died."

He didn't realize he'd been telling the story out loud until that moment. He didn't realize her hand was twined with his, gripping his fingers tightly.

"It wasn't your fault," she told him.

Everyone told him that. A part of him knew it, logically.

But a part of him just didn't believe it. It was his job to protect, and he hadn't been able to protect them. He hadn't been able to protect *anyone*.

"I quit the border patrol the next day," he said.

Her hand squeezed his.

They sat in silence for a long moment, while he waited for the images to fade from before his eyes. The wind didn't chill him anymore, because he was already stone cold.

"You need help to heal," she told him.

"I'm fine," he ground out.

"Your frustrations are eating away at you from the inside."

It did feel like acid, burning a bigger and bigger hole in his gut, but he didn't tell her that.

"You don't have to go to a counselor," she said. "But maybe a pastor. Pastor Lewis is—"

"I'm fine." He shot to his feet, letting go of her hand. Somehow, he felt smaller without it.

Monica rose more slowly. "Just think about it."

He didn't need to. He wasn't ready to talk to anyone. He didn't need to talk to anyone.

He could handle it himself.

Shaun had closed himself off from her, and it was her own fault.

Monica glanced at him as he drove his Suburban through downtown Sonoma, heading out toward San Francisco. She'd wanted him with her today because she had an appointment with her accountant about the clinic, and it would be sure to upset the stalker. But Shaun's silence and the subtle way he kept himself at arm's length from her told her volumes about what he was feeling.

"Still no notes from the stalker?" he asked.

"None," she said. It was ridiculous how her pulse jumped at his voice, at the realization that he was speaking to her.

Since the moment in Union Square Park, he'd only spoken to her when she'd asked him a question or he'd wanted her to do something.

When he had been telling her about the coyote, the pain etched across his face had broken her heart. He had spoken in a monotone, as if he didn't realize he was speaking out loud. This was a dark place inside him, and he needed healing.

She wanted to heal him.

And in hearing how the deaths of those people had affected him, she had also started to realize something for herself.

She knew it hadn't been that often, but it had seemed like the Emergency Room where she worked had always gotten trauma cases of policemen and firemen injured in the line of duty. She had seen the men's wives in their grief and brokenness when their husbands died in the Emergency Room. Their pain had been so deep, it had cut through Monica even though she'd only been the nurse, not the spouse. She had vowed she wouldn't put herself in a place where she would have to endure that.

But as she heard the horrible things Shaun had had to witness and endure, all by himself, she suddenly realized that those men needed their wives to be there for them, to help them heal. Shaun could have used someone to hold him, to help him release his frustration and anger, to force him to talk to a counselor. Instead, his feelings had festered and made him hollow with guilt.

Monica admitted she had never really been in love. But now she could see how love would make a woman risk the ultimate pain in order to share in the ultimate intimacy. She still wasn't sure if she herself could do it, but she understood it now.

They were on a main street, with no stoplights but with several small side streets. Shaun slowed down.

"What is it?" she asked.

"Nothing serious. It's just that sometimes people shoot out of these side streets without looking."

As he spoke, he had turned his head to look down a side street they were passing, and Monica followed his gaze in time to see the dark shadow of a pickup truck fill her vision.

She didn't even have time to scream.

Shaun hit the brakes and yanked the wheel. The Suburban skidded out of the way of the oncoming pickup, which had been on target to hit them square in the side. Instead, it rammed into the edge of their bumper with a jarring crunch.

The airbags deployed just as the Suburban shuddered to a halt. The slap of the bag against her face sent her head backward.

"Are you okay?" Shaun asked.

"I'm fine…" She looked out his rear window. The pickup truck, after missing them, had apparently swerved around to avoid slamming into a bank and was now heading toward them again. "Shaun!"

He stepped on the gas and jerked the Suburban out of the way of the oncoming truck, then zoomed down the street.

Monica turned to look behind him. "He's after us." The truck was a newer model with a strong engine. He could have moved up alongside them, but instead he hung back and slightly to their left.

"He's trying to do the PIT maneuver on us," Shaun said, looking into his side view mirror. "Hang on." He gunned the engine and aimed straight for a lamppost.

"Shaun!"

At the last second, he swerved the Suburban out of the way.

However, the pickup had been focusing on trying to ram them and didn't notice in time—it hit the lamppost straight on.

The crunch of metal grated in her ears as Shaun's driving slammed her against the side of the Suburban. Then he slowed the car and pulled over onto the side of the road. He unbuckled his seatbelt and opened the door.

"What are you doing?" she said.

Shaun raced back down the street toward the pickup truck, but Monica could see a dark figure crawl out of the ruined truck and run away. He was too far ahead of Shaun, but maybe he could narrow the distance between them.

Then she noticed that several other cars had crashed as a result of the pickup's wild pursuit. She immediately got out of the Suburban and raced to the nearest vehicle. "Are you all right?" Monica asked the young woman who was stumbling out of a minivan. "Are your kids okay?"

"I hadn't picked them up yet, thank God," the woman said, pressing a hand to her temple. "I'm all right."

Monica didn't see any blood, but she told the woman to sit down on the curb nearby. She reached into her pockets and realized she'd left her phone in the Suburban, so she asked the woman, "Do you have a cell phone? Can you call the police?"

Monica went from person to person until the police and an ambulance arrived, comforting a shaking gray-haired woman and helping to stop the bleeding of a minor abrasion on a teenage girl. She didn't think, she just acted, going into nursing mode, saying the right things, working efficiently and gently.

And then as the paramedics arrived to check an old man with a tender ankle, she felt a hand on her shoulder and saw Shaun standing there, clutching his side and breathing heavily.

She burst into tears.

His arms went around her like bands of steel, holding her close. She was shaking. She was probably in shock. But

Shaun's solid presence helped her to calm down quickly after that release of emotions.

Unlike the last time she'd cried on his shoulder, when her tears stopped, he gently stepped back. He held her shoulders at arm's length away from him, and it seemed like a chasm.

"You're okay," he said to her.

She nodded numbly.

"I'm going to go talk to the officer," he said. "You'll be okay here?"

"I'm fine," she croaked.

She watched him walk away. He had saved her life. He had pushed her away.

And she realized she loved him.

Monica squinted at the fuzzy video of the man getting out of the wrecked pickup truck. She turned to Detective Carter. "That's the best video you could get of him?"

"We're lucky we got video at all," the detective replied, leaning back against the table in the Sonoma Police Department audio/visual room. "The place where he would have T-boned you doesn't have any cameras, but since he missed you there, he had to chase you and he got in range of this camera on the office building down the street from the crash."

She leaned in to look at the video again. "I can't tell who it is at all."

"When I was chasing him, I could tell he was about Phillip Bromley's height," Shaun said. He sat back in his chair and crossed his arms.

Monica shook her head. "Look at the way this man moves. He doesn't quite seem like Phillip." She glanced at Detective Carter. "Did you talk to Phillip?" They'd told him what Phillip had confessed to them a few days earlier.

"I did yesterday. He said the same thing you did." He

looked at her squarely. "I'm looking into it, Monica. I'm not sure yet if he's telling the truth or not."

The detective turned to Shaun. "You said the man had a car near the intersection where he was going to T-bone you?"

Shaun nodded. "It was parked down Elm Street. When I chased him, he was too far ahead of me. He got into the car and took off."

"I ran the license plate number you gave me," Detective Carter said. "The man's getaway car was stolen only that morning, same as the pickup truck."

Shaun sighed.

"You got DNA off the steering wheel of the pickup, right?" Monica asked.

"We sent it to the lab. They did a quick screening and it looks like it might be the same DNA from Shaun's attacker, but it'll take another week to be sure. If it is the same person, we know his DNA isn't in any of the databases."

Monica and Shaun thanked the detective and left the station, but as she stepped out onto the sidewalk, she suddenly felt vulnerable and open. She looked around at the busy streets of downtown Sonoma, filled with tourists.

"What is it?" Shaun asked. "Do you see him?"

"No. I just think I do." She walked quickly toward Shaun's car, a small loaner sedan while the garage repaired his Suburban. "I got photos this morning." Candids taken a few days ago, again with the red bull's-eye drawn over her face. "I liked it better when I didn't know if he was watching me and taking photos or not."

Her cell phone rang as they were passing a group of young Hispanic men loitering at the corner of the hardware store, and she had to walk quickly to move out of range of their chatter.

It was Phillip Bromley. "Hi, Phillip."

Shaun frowned at her. She turned her back to him.

"Monica, I, uh, I need to talk to you."

"I'm afraid I'm a bit busy—"

"It won't take more than a minute. I'm in Sonoma right now."

"You're here?" She glanced around. "Where?"

"I'm at Lorianne's Café."

"We're only a couple blocks away. We'll meet you there."

Shaun's lips were pressed together as he watched her put her phone away. "The man could be a stalker and a murderer."

She hesitated, then she said slowly, "I don't think he is."

"What? Why would you believe him?"

"I can't explain it." She began walking toward the café. "When I was watching him, my gut said that he was telling the truth about seeing that man outside of Clare's townhouse."

"It was pretty convenient, don't you think? Especially since he's the only one who saw him."

"Did Nathan's friend in the LAPD ever find that convenience store clerk and show him Phillip's photo?"

Shaun scowled. "Not yet. They can't find him because he quit the store a few years ago."

"Until he positively identifies the man wearing the duster as Phillip, there's no way to know for sure if Phillip is lying or telling the truth." She stopped and looked Shaun in the eye. "You can believe he's lying. Fine. But I'm going to believe he's telling the truth. There's no difference between us. We're both choosing to believe something without proof."

He had a stunned look on his face, but she turned and kept walking toward the café.

Inside, she spotted Phillip sitting at the bar, but he wasn't drinking anything. His expression was serious as he greeted her. He seemed worried.

He held something out in his hand, and she automatically reached for it. It was a flashdrive.

"After I talked to you, I started to think back to the time

I spent with Clare in L.A., and people we both knew or saw. So I dug up some old digital photos on my computer."

Monica's heart started to beat faster.

Phillip continued, "I think I saw the same guy in the background at three different places, on three different days. In two of the pictures, he has a camera in his hand."

A camera? Monica's hand closed securely over the flash-drive. "Are the photos dated?"

"I downloaded them from my digital camera on different days over a three month period. Just look at the date of the file to see when it was created."

"Did you recognize the man?" Shaun asked. Monica had almost forgotten about him. He had a tight edge to his voice as he spoke, as if he wasn't sure if he wanted to be sarcastic or earnest in his question.

Phillip shook his head. "I've never seen him before, which makes it strange that he'd be at those three parties. We usually knew all the people who went to the same parties."

"Thank you, Phillip," Monica said.

"Don't thank me yet. I don't take very good pictures, especially after I've had a few drinks."

"Anything is better than nothing."

He headed toward the door to the restaurant, but then he paused and looked back at her. "Even if I don't do anything else in my life," he said fervently, "I wanted to help you catch this guy. I wanted to do something that I would be really proud of."

And then he turned and walked away.

TWELVE

Monica frowned at her laptop computer screen and reflected that Phillip Bromley really did take terrible pictures.

Shaun scooted his chair closer to her at the kitchen table, where Monica had set up her laptop. Behind them, Evita was preparing lunch at the stove, and the smell of fajitas filled the air.

Phillip had included all the photos he'd shot during the months when Clare had been in L.A. Some of them were of the same party Clare had gone to, but not all the pictures included her in it.

But he'd put three pictures in a folder to single them out, and it did indeed look like the same man was in the background of all three.

One was a shot of Clare with her roommate at a restaurant, posing for Phillip's camera. Over Clare's left shoulder was a dark-skinned man sitting at a table behind the two girls. He had dark blond hair that contrasted with his skin. On the table was a camera.

The second picture had been taken in a nightclub, and the camera's flash had blinded out much of the three people Phillip had been taking a picture of. One of them was Clare, one was her boyfriend, the third was a girl Shaun didn't recognize. Between Clare and her boyfriend's heads could be seen the figure of a man leaning against a pillar. The photo was very fuzzy even when they blew it up on the computer screen, but something about the way he held his head, positioned his shoulders, seemed like the man in the first photo. The nightclub was dark and they couldn't see much of him.

The last photo was of Phillip sitting down in a movie theater with Clare at his right. He had taken the picture himself—his left arm stretched to the side of the picture to show where he'd held the camera out in front of them to take the shot, but he hadn't been centered, and the picture showed only half of Clare's face cut off by the edge of the photo.

But because of Phillip's bad shot, the majority of the photo showed the rows of chairs behind them. And directly over Phillip's left shoulder, a few rows back, was a man.

It was the least blurry of the three pictures, but even then, the man's features weren't very clear. He had an oval face, tanned skin and long, wavy hair that was a darkish blond color. His eyes might have seemed a little close together because they were small for his face, but since the shot was head-on, it was hard to tell if his nose was big or not.

Monica stared at him. "Something about him seems familiar, but I can't place him. I don't think he looks like any of my investors."

"I don't think so, either." Shaun leaned in so he could stare at the picture, and it brought his face close to hers. Her skin prickled at his nearness, and she scooted her body away from him.

The man in the third picture was almost definitely the same man as the one in the first picture, and possibly in the second picture, too.

"He looks like a day worker." Evita laid a hot plate of fajita-grilled chicken in front of them.

"You mean Hispanic?" Monica asked her.

"Not just that, but he looks like one of the migrant workers or one of the field laborers."

"How can you tell?" Shaun asked.

Evita pointed her spatula at the computer screen. "Look at his eyes. No raccoon eyes tan lines. Because they wear sunglasses, a tourist or an athlete will usually have a band around the eyes that's lighter than their tan. But day laborers don't since they don't usually have sunglasses."

She was right. The man's face was very evenly darkened. "You don't think he's just naturally dark-skinned?"

Evita shrugged. "He could be, but he'd be a little dark for a Hispanic man. When I first looked at him, I thought he looked tanned."

"I think he is tanned," Shaun said. "Look at the dates on these pictures. This one, where his skin is darkest, was taken only a couple of weeks after Clare moved to L.A. These two pictures were two and three months later, and his skin looks a lot lighter."

"So he was tanned when he was up here in Sonoma, when he first started stalking Clare," Monica said. "He was a day laborer somewhere in this area."

"I don't think that helps us any," Shaun said. "There are hundreds of migrant workers and field laborers in Sonoma county."

"But he had to have been working close to Clare. Let me call Rachel's boyfriend Edward. He hires field laborers for both his greenhouses and also his mother's farm. It's a long-shot, but I can't think of anything else."

She dialed the number for Edward's greenhouse business, which was his cell phone number. He picked up on the first ring. "Hi, Monica."

"Edward, I hope you don't mind, but I have a favor to ask. I have some five-year-old pictures of a man who had been a day laborer in Sonoma. Do you know if there's a way to find out if anyone knew this guy?"

Edward blew out a breath. "I doubt it, but let me talk to some of my guys and ask. The laborer community is pretty tight-knit, so they might be able to remember someone from five years ago. But I can't promise you anything."

"That's fine. It's the only thing I can think of to find out who this guy is."

"I'll call you later."

Even before she'd disconnected the call, the doorbell rang urgently over and over again. Monica and Shaun left the kitchen and headed into the foyer. A quick glance in the video monitor revealed Detective Carter, whom they let into the house immediately. His expression was dark and forbidding as he saw them.

"Phillip Bromley was just found dead in his car, and you two were the last to see him alive."

The carpet had been yanked out from under him.

Shaun woke up early to the predawn stillness. But the first thing he thought of was Phillip Bromley.

Innocent.

Dead.

The detective had said that Phillip had been hit in the face, maybe from a fist, and the blow had broken his nose. He'd parked in a small gravel lot a block away from the restaurant so no one had seen him. There had been signs that a man had struggled with him, throwing Phillip down onto his hands and knees in front of his driver's side door. Phillip had been forced into the front seat of the car, the attacker in the backseat.

And the attacker had strangled Phillip with a belt.

A crime of opportunity. Shaun stared at his bedroom ceiling and his throat tightened at the thought. He almost felt as if a belt were looped around his own neck.

At first, Shaun had thought the stalker must have somehow known Phillip was handing Monica the thumbdrive of photos, but he couldn't figure out how the stalker would have found out. Then Monica had pointed out that if Phillip had been looking through the photos, he had been staring at the face of the stalker. If Phillip happened to run into him on the streets of Sonoma, there was a chance he would have recognized the man.

And the stalker would have seen that Phillip knew him.

Shaun could almost imagine the scenario. Phillip sees the man and is surprised and fearful. The man realizes Phillip recognizes him and punches him in the face to disorient him, drags him to the car. Shoves him into the front seat while he's still dazed. Gets into the backseat, removes his belt, and strangles him.

For so long, Shaun had thought that Phillip was Clare's stalker, and now it looked like he'd been wrong all along. Terribly wrong. Monica had seen that Phillip was telling the truth about the other man at Clare's doorstep that night, but Shaun had only wanted Phillip to be guilty.

He had been so blinded by his desire to right the wrong done to Clare that he hadn't been able to see the truth. He'd only seen what he wanted to see. He'd wanted to feel the anger and let it drive him. He'd thought it was anger at Phillip, anger at the injustice, but in reality, it had been anger at himself. Monica had been right.

Shaun sat up in bed and watched the sun rise over the rolling foothills from his bedroom window. He automatically reached for the Bible on his nightstand.

He read his Bible almost every day, although lately it had been more like a duty than anything else. He wondered, now, if maybe that had been because God had been trying to tell him that his heart needed adjusting.

Or healing.

He turned to where he'd left off reading yesterday, and found himself at Psalm seventy-four. But today, somehow, the passage seemed more alive. The words leaped off the page at him.

We are given no signs from God; no prophets are left, and none of us knows how long this will be.

He had felt like that, that day watching the van sink below the waters. The coyote had swum to the opposite shore and stopped to watch. He had laughed and jeered at them all before running away.

As Shaun had surfaced from his last dive and realized he couldn't save those people, he had thought, Where was God?

But God is my King from long ago; He brings salvation on the earth.

And verse twenty-two:

Rise up, O God, and defend your cause; remember how fools mock you all day long.

The coyote's jeering echoed in his head, but the verses seemed to also be shouting at him to remember that it was God who was his King. God who brought salvation. God who would rise up and defend his cause.

God. Not Shaun.

He had thought he should be able to save those people, just like he thought he should be able to protect all the other innocents he'd come across on the border patrol, and Clare. He should have protected them.

Him, Shaun. Not God.

It's why he'd been so angry—he'd wanted to protect them. He couldn't. So the anger took root, and turned into a driving force that made him focus too much energy at Phillip Bromley.

The young clerk at Captain Caffeine's Espresso shop had mentioned the man was tanned. Monica herself had asked why Phillip would bother to stalk Clare and send her threatening notes when they had hung out with the same crowd of people. There had been so many discrepancies like the fact that Phillip had never smelled like that distinctive brand of cigarette but Shaun had focused only on the black leather duster and general physical similarities.

Lord, forgive me. Please help me to let it go.

But even as he prayed it, he realized he was still thinking he could do it himself.

Lord, heal me.

Monica had mentioned Pastor Lewis from their church. Maybe it was time to unburden himself with someone he could trust, who could help him make sense of the darkness he felt.

Lord, heal me.

And Shaun knew He would.

Monica knew something inside Shaun had changed as soon as she answered the front door to him. She wanted to ask him about it, but mindful of her family having breakfast in the kitchen, she only said, "Thanks for coming so early. Did you want breakfast?"

He shook his head. "I was up early and ate already. Are you ready to go?"

She nodded, and followed him out to his car. "Edward said that he'd go get Jorge and bring him to his greenhouses by six-thirty."

Yesterday, Edward had talked to the field hands he hired to work his mother's farm, and surprisingly they'd all said that if anyone would remember a man from five years ago, it would be old Jorge. In his younger years, he had been a farm worker who worked many of the fields across Sonoma, but then he and his wife started a business making burritos and going to the various fields at lunchtime to sell the food cheaply to the laborers. They made a nice enough profit that they started their own tavern just outside of Sonoma, with a lunch wagon they still sent out to the various fields to sell cheap lunches. Edward's field workers said that Jorge knew practically all the workers in Sonoma county, and what was more, he had a sharp memory and a knack of remembering people's names.

Edward had called her yesterday to set up a time to meet with Jorge this morning. Jorge needed to meet with them early so he'd have time to get back to the tavern and get ready for the lunch crowd.

However, if the stalker followed Monica to visit Jorge at his tavern, he'd know they were on to him. So Monica had asked Edward to pick up Jorge and bring him to the greenhouse before she and Shaun arrived there.

Shaun drove cautiously even though the roads were mostly deserted.

"What's wrong?" she asked.

"I'm probably just paranoid. Ever since getting hit, I feel vulnerable in this little car." He knocked on the dashboard of the sedan. "I can't wait to get my Suburban back from the garage. I feel safer in it."

They arrived at the greenhouses in only a few minutes and headed into the office. An older Hispanic man was sitting in the chair across from Edward's desk, and he rose to greet them.

"Hallo," he said.

"Hi, Jorge," Monica said. "Thanks for meeting with us."

Jorge's hand was calloused and strong when she shook it, and he had a wide smile that creased his tanned face with deep laugh lines. "Such a pretty girl, I not say no." He had a thick accent.

Shaun also shook his hand, and the man regarded him with searching eyes. He nodded to Shaun as if he approved of what he saw.

Edward gestured to two other chairs, then sat back down behind his desk. "If you're okay with it, I'll translate for Jorge. He's already said it's fine with him."

"I can speak Spanish," Shaun said to Edward, "but you're still welcome to stay." He pulled out the three pictures they'd printed on his father's photo printer and showed them to Jorge, speaking to him rapidly in Spanish.

Jorge's eyes searched the pictures, frowning as he studied them. Monica's hopes began to dwindle. She had hoped for some light of recognition from him, but knew the odds had been against it.

Jorge replied to Shaun, although his answer was longer than a simple, "No, I don't recognize this man." Monica waited for Shaun to translate for her, trying to still the nervous tapping of her foot.

Shaun turned to her, but his face was grim. "Jorge says he does recognize the man's face, but he doesn't know much about him."

"Not even his name?"

"He says he did know his first name, and he's trying to remember it. It's on the tip of his tongue but he can't quite get it. But he didn't know his last name."

Just a first name wasn't much help to them. Monica squelched a sigh.

Shaun continued, "At the time, Jorge heard some of the other men talk about this guy a little. They said he kept to himself. He wasn't consistent about being available for work. Most men will hang out at certain street corners in the mornings to wait for contractors to drive by and hire them on the spot just for the day. This guy wasn't out there every day."

"He was probably following Clare," Monica murmured.

"He doesn't know anything else about him—" Jorge interrupted Shaun with a spate of Spanish, and Shaun said, "Jorge says this guy had brown hair when he was in Sonoma."

And in the pictures he was dirty blond. Had he dyed it when he was in Sonoma and then changed it back in L.A.? Or was he naturally brown-haired and he dyed it blond when he moved down south?

Shaun asked Jorge something, and Jorge shook his head. Shaun said, "He doesn't remember anything else about him."

Monica tried not to let her disappointment show on her face, but Jorge must have seen it, because he reached out to take her hand. "Sorry, eh?" he said. He said something in Spanish, and Edward laughed.

"Jorge says that there are lots of other cuter guys for you, like us two," Edward told Monica.

She smiled at the older man. "Thank you."

"De nada," he replied. You're welcome.

Edward rose to his feet. "I need to get Jorge back to the tavern or else his wife will get at him for shirking work."

"Wait a few minutes after we leave before you take him back," Shaun said. "If the stalker followed us, then he won't see that we talked to Jorge."

Shaun thanked the two men and he and Monica left the office. She didn't say much on the ride back home. What was there to say? Another dead end. She'd been so hopeful when she saw Phillip's photos.

At one point she asked him, "Are you all right?"

He opened his mouth, closed it, then said, "I'm fine."

It was a door politely but firmly shut in her face. She couldn't blame him. He was processing a lot of information. Phillip's death must have been a blow to him, and yet he didn't seem depressed or frustrated. He also didn't seem angry anymore. She wanted to let him know she was there for him, but she couldn't do that, because he'd made it clear he didn't want her.

She had to get used to that fact.

Once they got back to her house, she told him, "I'll be staying home today."

"If you need to go somewhere, let me know," he said.

After she'd gone inside the house, she stood and watched his car drive away.

"Monica."

Her aunt's voice behind her made her jump and turn guiltily. She was acting like a teenager.

Aunt Becca held out an envelope. "This came for you at the spa yesterday. I forgot to give it to you when I heard about Phillip Bromley."

She sometimes got mail at the spa—both legitimate and junk mail—from people who didn't know her San Francisco address or her Sonoma post office box number, whereas the spa address was easy to find on the internet or the phone book. "Oh, maybe it's my clinic's business plan. My hospital administrator friend was supposed to send me another…" Her voice trailed off as she realized the envelope had no return address.

A fist squeezed her heart. She would have thought by now she'd be used to getting these horrible things.

"Monica?" Aunt Becca took a step closer. "What's wrong?"

"I need gloves." She was amazed at how calmly she said it, and she went to the library to get some gloves from the box next to the first-aid kit. Her aunt followed.

Monica gloved up and used a scalpel to slit open the envelope, the same thing she'd been doing for all the photos she'd received. She upended the envelope onto a side table next to a leather chair.

A picture of her sister Naomi's face stared up at her.

Aunt Becca gasped.

Monica's chest began to hurt, and she vaguely wondered if she was having a heart attack. She pressed her hand hard above her heart and felt the rapid beating.

She had to breathe. She forced her diaphragm to expand, then contract. Then again. She finally felt steady enough to reach down to pick up the stack of photos.

The pictures were all of her family. Aunt Becca, Naomi, Rachel, her father. All taken outside from the past several days. He'd been following her family and taking pictures of them.

Another note had been tucked in with the pictures.

If you care about them, you'll stop what you're doing.

A cry escaped her lips, and the note fell to the floor. What had she done? Why had she been so determined not to let this man control her that she put her own family at risk? What was wrong with her?

What kind of a person had she become?

Her knees gave way, and she collapsed onto the floor.

"Monica!" Aunt Becca bent down to reach for her.

Monica squeezed her eyes shut. She wanted to curl into a ball. Her fingers dug into the carpet.

"Monica." Aunt Becca's voice sounded right in her ear, and she opened her eyes to realize that her aunt had sat on the floor with her.

"I can't let him hurt you," she said.

"I know, honey." Aunt Becca smoothed back Monica's hair.

"Why didn't I see this coming?" Monica's throat began to close up. "Why did I insist on doing this? I wanted to flush him out, I wanted to catch him. And I put my family at risk. What does that say about who I am?"

"Monica…"

"Everything is falling apart. My investors won't want to

touch the clinic after Phillip's death comes out. My family is being threatened. My clinic will never happen." Tears spilled out of her eyes, but she dashed them away impatiently. "I don't understand why this is happening. Isn't my free children's clinic a worthwhile project? Why wouldn't God want to bless this project? Why are there so many problems?"

"Maybe He just wants you to postpone it for a little while."

"Or maybe He's trying to tell me that Dad was right, that I can't do anything worthwhile."

Aunt Becca's voice grew firm. "God would never say that to you."

"But why else would He put so many roadblocks in the way of something so important? It's not the clinic, so it's got to be me."

"Monica, listen to me." Aunt Becca took her hand. "Why are you doing this project?"

"Because there's a need in Sonoma county."

"But why Sonoma? Why not somewhere else?"

"Uh…" It had seemed a natural place to have a children's clinic. She hadn't even considered putting it anywhere else.

"I think you put it in Sonoma because you feel the need to prove something to yourself," Aunt Becca said. "I think that you believe this clinic will make you feel significant."

The word struck a chord inside her. "I don't know what you're talking about. I'm signifi—" Her voice trailed off. She couldn't say it. "I always feel out of place. I wanted to forge my own way, but it always made Dad mad at me."

"I know he doesn't quite understand you, but he only wants what's best for you. Unfortunately, his idea of what's best isn't always really what's best."

"What is what's best? At the hospital, I was a good worker bee, but I wanted to put my hands on something that would make an impact."

But then it all became clear to her. She believed that if the clinic made an impact, maybe then her *father* would realize she had done something good, something worthwhile, something…significant.

"I want the clinic because I think it will make Dad respect me," she said in a small voice.

"Oh, Monica." Aunt Becca put her arms around her. "I think you need to realize that Jesus already respects you."

Already? Despite the fact she hadn't done anything big for Him?

"Jesus loves you, and His love makes you worthwhile. When you follow God's will for you, you're valued not because of what specifically you're doing. You're valued because you're doing God's work."

"But wouldn't God think a free children's clinic is better than me just being a nurse?"

"You can feel important even just being a resident nurse at your father's spa, if that's what God's purpose is for you. You need to obey God and find your worth in Him, not in your father's approval or in what you accomplish in this world."

She didn't know what to say in response to that. But what she did know was that the clinic wasn't worth the risk to her family.

How had it become so important to her in the first place?

Aunt Becca got to her feet with a soft *oomph.* "My knees just aren't the same these days." She laid a hand on Monica's shoulder. "Why don't you pray about it?" And then she left the library, closing the door behind her.

Monica remained on the floor, feeling dazed, drained and yet relieved at the same time. She finally understood what had been at the root of all she'd been feeling, and understanding it made it better, somehow.

She closed her eyes, folded her hands, and bowed her head. *Lord, what do You want me to do?*

THIRTEEN

"Dad." Monica entered her father's bedroom.

He looked up from where he sat in the recliner in front of the fireplace. His Bible was open in his lap. His eyes seemed tired as they looked at her. "Come in. Sit down."

She sat in the chair opposite his, her heart beating slow and steady. She was surprised at how calm she felt. "Dad, I'm sorry for worrying you."

He didn't look at her, but he didn't seem upset. Maybe embarrassed.

"I'm stopping the free clinic project."

Now he did look at her. "Are you sure? What brought this about?"

"I got a note threatening my family. You all are more important than a clinic."

Much more important than her need to feel significant. She also had to trust that God would protect her family against this madman.

"So…" He fingered the edges of his Bible. "What are you going to do when I don't need you anymore? Go back to the hospital in San Francisco?"

"I'll stay and work as resident nurse at the spa." The words came out easier than she had expected them to.

She had thought her father would be rejoicing, but he looked at her in confusion. "I don't understand."

"I was praying, and I felt God wants me to put my family first."

"And so…just like that? You set aside your plans for the clinic?"

"Willingly." Without bitterness or anger or reluctance. Instead, she felt peace knowing God was pleased that she was obeying His purpose for her, even though it wasn't what she had imagined for herself.

"What about what you were saying about the need in Sonoma?" he asked.

"There's still a need, but I feel like God doesn't want me to fill it right now with my clinic. He wants me at the spa."

"I…I'm glad." But his voice seemed more shocked than happy.

"I knew you would be. That's why I came to tell you." She rose and kissed his cheek. "I'll see you this afternoon for your appointment, Dad."

She went to the breakfast room where Naomi and Aunt Becca were lingering over coffee. "Where's Rachel?" she asked.

"She left for the spa already," Naomi said.

Monica stilled. She hadn't had time to think about if it might be dangerous for her sisters to be traveling alone right now. In fact, Aunt Becca got the envelope yesterday in the mail, which meant the stalker sent the threat to her family the day before. Which meant it was the next day that he killed Phillip Bromley.

Aunt Becca caught her eye. "I didn't even think if it would be safe for her."

"What do you mean, safe?" Naomi asked.

"The stalker sent photos of you guys and threatened to

hurt you," Monica said. "I've…" She sighed. "I've decided to stop work on the clinic."

"Oh, Monica." Naomi reached out to grab her hand. "I know how much it means to you."

"I'm okay with it, really. I think it's what God wants me to do."

"In the meantime, we should probably be a bit more cautious," Aunt Becca said. "I can call Detective Carter—"

"No, I'll call Shaun. He can drive you all to the spa this morning."

"I was going to ask you if you could come to the spa to help out this morning," Naomi said. "I have three interviews set up with potential spa managers to take over when I get married, so Aunt Becca and I will be busy with those. Do you mind watching over things?"

"Not at all." She'd have to get used to the way the spa was run, anyway, if she was going to work there. She dialed Shaun's number.

"Hi," he said.

"The stalker sent photos of my family to the spa yesterday, with a note that said he'd hurt them if I didn't stop."

"He sent them to the spa? Not your house?"

"He addressed the envelope to me in care of Aunt Becca. I think he did it to rattle me, to let me know he could get to her. Or maybe he wanted Aunt Becca to open it." Monica was glad her aunt hadn't thought twice about the envelope or been tempted to open it. "So in light of all that, I've decided to cancel the clinic project. I'm also going to do what Dad wants and work as resident nurse at the spa."

He was silent a long moment. "Are you sure about this?"

"I feel it's what God wants me to do."

"You know I supported you in your free children's clinic, right?"

"I know."

"But I think it's good for you to do this to protect your family. And I think it's a good idea for you to work for your dad. You're putting your family first and it'll lead to stronger family ties that will make up for any disappointment of not fulfilling your dream for the clinic."

His affirmation was a buoy in open waters, and she clung to it. "Thanks."

"I know you don't get along well with your dad, but maybe this will help you improve things."

"Yeah, it probably will." And she realized she wanted the kind of relationship with her father that Shaun had with his.

"So what's next?" he asked.

She was surprised he wasn't more disappointed in losing the chance of finding his sister's killer by drawing him out. It was unlike Shaun, but then she remembered how changed he'd been earlier this morning when they went to visit Jorge and wondered again what had happened. "I have to call my investors later today to tell them I'm canceling the project, and hopefully the stalker will find out."

And leave her alone.

And stalk some other woman.

No, she couldn't think like that. She had to trust God. She knew this was what He wanted her to do.

"In the meantime, I want to protect my family. Can you pick us up and take us to the spa? I'm going there to help Naomi today."

"Sure."

"You don't need to stick around. The spa has outside video surveillance and security guards."

"Of course I'll stick around," Shaun said.

He picked them up a little while later, but as they turned out of the driveway, Monica felt a shiver walk across her shoulder blades. Was the stalker watching them or was she being paranoid?

When they arrived at the spa, Shaun drove to the back and parked. They entered through the back door, but Monica held Shaun's arm and let Naomi and Aunt Becca continue down the hallway toward their offices.

"Are you all right?" she asked.

There was a brief flash on his face, a rush of raw emotion that she hadn't seen in him before. And she could see that it frightened him.

The next moment, he'd closed himself up and said, "I'm fine."

She had the feeling he was pushing her away because he was dealing with something so sore and sensitive, he didn't know how to share it with anyone. She didn't think he was pushing her away because of anything she'd done, but it still hurt.

He said, "The spa is close to the garage. I'm going to see if my Suburban is ready yet. I'll be back in a few minutes. You'll be okay here, right?"

"I can barricade myself in the security guards' room if you want." She tried to be light-hearted about it, but it sounded harsh in her ears.

"I'll be back." He left through the back door.

Monica went looking for her aunt and found her in the front foyer of the spa. There were already several patrons waiting to be served at the receptionist's desk.

"Monica, can you help Jenny and Iona?" Aunt Becca said, referring to the two receptionists. "I have to get ready for my first interview."

"Sure."

Aunt Becca disappeared through the double doors leading into the main area of the spa, and Monica approached a woman standing next in line. "How can I help you?"

The woman needed to check in for her appointment, so Monica did that for her and then stood chatting with her until

Haley entered the foyer. "Mrs. Higley, this is Haley, and she'll take you in back for your facial."

Her cell phone rang. "Hi, Dad."

"Monica, an envelope came for you this morning in the mail."

"Don't open it, Dad, at least not without gloves. We'll give it to Detective Carter later."

"Are you sure? It's rather large."

"How large?" she asked.

"Well, let me see…"

Then the front door to the spa opened. Monica looked up and saw a man with tanned skin approaching her.

It was as if it were happening in slow motion. As he walked toward her it was as if he took a minute for each step he took. At first she didn't realize who she was looking at because his face was much thinner than it had been in the L.A. photos. Also, his hair was shorter and more brown than blond, a very expensive highlighting job, and he had on a suit and tie rather than the casual open-necked shirts he wore in the pictures.

Then it dawned on her that this was Clare's stalker. This was her stalker.

And in another split second, she realized that this was Rodney Lassiter.

He was even more tanned than when she'd done the video chat with him, and in the chat, he'd been wearing sunglasses. Now that he didn't have those glasses on, she saw that his small eyes were set close to his long nose, and like in the photos from five years ago, he again had no sunglass tan line across his eyes. His narrow face made his nose look larger than it was.

If he dressed in a T-shirt, jeans, and workboots, he'd look like a local field worker. In downtown Sonoma, or just hanging around the countryside, he'd blend in perfectly.

Here, at the spa, he again blended in with his expensive suit, his diamond-crusted watch, his Italian leather shoes. No one gave him a second glance except for Monica.

She whipped her head around and opened her mouth to tell someone to call the police, but Rodney was suddenly there, pressed up against her side, his cigarette smoke choking her. He grabbed her cell phone away from her.

And a sharp object stuck hard into her side.

At first she thought it was a knife. Could she fight him off with some of the jiujitsu moves Shaun had taught her? Her hands shook. She tried to remember the moves, but her mind whirled with nothing but random images.

Then he moved closer to her, his other hand grabbing her arm, pressing the object deeper under her ribcage as he whispered in her ear, "Say anything and I'll shoot you."

A gun.

"You're going to come with me right now," he said.

Iona had finished speaking with the patron she'd been dealing with and noticed Rodney standing beside Monica. "Hello, sir, how can I help you?"

"I just need to speak to Monica for a moment," he answered in a smooth, calm voice, but the gun jabbed at her.

He was going to take her, and he would kill her. Maybe he'd make it look like suicide, or maybe he'd just kill her outright like he did with Phillip. Either way, he'd get what he wanted—she'd be dead, and his identity would die with her.

She couldn't let that happen. She couldn't let him go free to hurt more people.

He was threatening to kill her now, but he'd definitely kill her if he took her. If she said something now, he'd shoot her but they would at least know the stalker was Rodney Lassiter, not some nameless migrant worker.

She began hyperventilating. *Calm down. You have to do this.*

At that moment, Aunt Becca entered the foyer again, looking down at some papers in her hands.

"Monica, I need your opinion…" Aunt Becca looked up from her papers and saw Rodney. Saw Monica's face. Knew something was wrong.

Rodney raised his gun and shot her aunt.

The sound cracked in her ear and echoed fiercely through the high-ceilinged foyer, reverberating through the marble floors. Iona and Jenny and the few patrons in the room screamed and ducked.

Aunt Becca went down.

"No!"

Monica jerked forward to go to her aunt, but Rodney's grip on her arm was too strong. Suddenly she was being pulled backward, out of the spa, through the front doors. She tried to resist, but her limbs felt numb.

"Stay back!" Rodney ordered the valets out front, pointing the gun at them.

He'd left his car near the door. "Get in the driver's seat," he said. "And don't put on your seatbelt." At first she was confused, but then she realized that if she tried anything while driving, she wouldn't have as much control over the car without her seatbelt on.

She obeyed, and he got into the backseat.

"Drive."

Shaun sent up a fervent prayer thanking God that the stalker was a terrible shot.

He hovered over the paramedics as they took care of Becca, and he could see that the bullet had gone through her right shoulder. Her face was drawn and pale, but she looked alert and otherwise okay.

"Will she be okay?" Detective Carter asked the paramedics.

"She'll be fine, sir," one of them said.

After the stalker left with Monica, the receptionists had called the police and an ambulance. It was Detective Carter who had called Shaun, and he'd arrived at the spa only a few minutes after they did.

Shaun looked at the detective's tight jaw and creased brow and knew it was killing him to not be able to go to the hospital with Becca. But after going out to the ambulance with her, Detective Carter returned to the spa to talk to the other officers who had arrived with him, who had been talking to the witnesses.

The detective's cell phone rang. He looked at the caller ID, then ignored the call and continued to talk to the officers. Then he got a beep from a text message. Looking at it, he frowned, then made a phone call. "Edward."

Shaun headed closer to him at the sound of the name.

The detective's brows knit together as he listened to Edward. "Yes, he's…Jorge?…"

"Jorge?" Shaun said.

"Thank you, Edward." Detective Carter hung up and turned to Shaun. "Edward said he didn't have your phone number or he would have called you himself. Jorge called him—he remembered the name of the man in Phillip's photos. Emmanuel."

Emmanuel. Lots of Hispanic men had that name, it wasn't unusual or uncommon. But at least they had a name.

If it was even his real name.

Detective Carter approached the two receptionists for the spa, and Shaun followed close behind him. The detective didn't object.

"Iona, you told my officer about the man who took Monica. Had you seen him before?"

She shook her head. "He's never come to the spa before. He was about medium height—only a little taller than me, with brown hair with blond highlights. Really dark tan."

This wasn't helping. They were only describing a man he'd already seen in those photos.

"Any unusual facial features?" the detective asked.

"Um…"

Iona bit her lip as she thought, and then the other receptionist said, "He had small eyes."

Detective Carter nodded and noted it down in his notebook.

This was all too slow. Monica was heading farther and farther away with each minute. The detective had called for roadblocks in and out of Sonoma, but the stalker might have already passed them by the time the roadblocks were set up. Shaun tried to relax, but his legs twitched with nervous energy.

"His nose was kind of big," Iona said.

"What was he wearing?"

"Dark business suit. Expensive shoes…" Iona grimaced, trying to remember.

Then the other receptionist added, "He had a really expensive watch. It was full of diamonds."

Diamonds. He'd seen a watch with diamonds.

"Can I use your computer?" Shaun asked. He scooted behind the receptionist's desk and pulled up an internet browser. Then he did an image search for Rodney Lassiter.

He'd had sunglasses on when Shaun had last seen him, so he hadn't seen his eyes. And now that he thought about it, Shaun realized Lassiter could have flown to Florida just before the video chat with Monica, pretending he'd been there the entire time. It would have been easy to pay someone to make his Miami hotel room look like it was slept in.

A publicity photo of Rodney Lassiter came up.

It was the man in Phillip's photos.

Rodney now had darker hair and he'd lost weight, so it took Shaun a moment to recognize him. He imagined Phillip feeling the same jolt of surprise as he realized he was face-to-face with Clare's stalker. Clare's killer.

Shaun wouldn't let him kill Monica, not if he could help it.

"Who is that?" Detective Carter demanded.

"Rodney Lassiter," Shaun said. "One of Monica's investors. He's Emmanuel."

The detective got on the phone immediately, but Shaun only heard his tense voice, not the words. He stared at Lassiter's picture, the small dead eyes, the calm mouth.

"You'll never catch me."

"Yes, I will," Shaun said through gritted teeth.

Except he knew they had nothing. They didn't know where Lassiter was staying in Sonoma. They didn't know where he'd taken Monica. All they had was his name.

Yesterday he would have popped off like a rocket, urgent to do something. He felt the emotions roiling under his skin, but there was something invisible wrapped around him, holding him steady, keeping the frustration in check.

He bowed his head, leaning against the desk. *Oh, God.*

He drew in a deep breath.

God, I couldn't protect my sister or those people in the van. I couldn't do it. Now Monica's gone, and it's the same thing—I can't do it.

But I know I don't have to.

Please. Please protect her. Please help us find her.

He remembered the last time he'd seen her, the bleakness in her face as he backed away. He hadn't been able to reach out to her, not with his pain still so raw inside him. He'd always thought he'd have time later to talk to her, to mend things between them. Now he realized he'd fallen in love with her.

God, I'm willing to risk my heart to her, if You can just save her.

He needed to do the hardest thing he'd ever done in his life, and trust God.

Detective Carter called Lassiter's Miami hotel and had the security team search his room. They found nothing to point to a place he might have taken Monica, just clothes strewn around the room.

The minutes ticked by, and Shaun paced back and forth through the foyer of the spa, trying to think of anything he could do that might help them find her, and sending up prayers to God to keep her safe.

Then his cell phone rang, an unknown San Francisco number. For a wild moment, he was certain it was Rodney calling to gloat. "Hello?"

"It's, er...John Butler," said a gruff voice.

The private investigator Rodney had hired.

"I...I changed my mind."

"We know your client's real name now," Shaun told him.

"I know where he's staying," Butler said.

"What?" Shaun's heart slammed hard in his chest.

"He wasn't prompt with his last payment, so I managed to find out where he was staying. I ran him to ground and got my money."

"Where?" Shaun demanded.

"The Fontana Hotel in Marin."

Rodney had Monica drive out of Sonoma fast, but then he took her on a circuitous route that finally ended up in Marin, just north of San Francisco. She had tried to tell him she needed to use the bathroom, but he called her bluff and told her to hold it or go where she sat.

Then they drove up into the Fontana Hotel driveway. "Pull the car up to the valet," he said.

"The hotel has cameras," she said. "They'll find you."

"It doesn't matter. I won't be here long, thanks to you. You couldn't just come quietly."

She'd blown his cover. Otherwise, he could have slipped away and no one would have known the stalker was Rodney Lassiter, VP of a luxury foods distribution company.

"If you run, if you do anything, I won't shoot *you*. I'll shoot someone else," he said in a nasty voice. "Now walk into the hotel." He slipped his hand and the gun into his suit jacket pocket.

She hesitated. They were a few feet from the front doors, and a valet was already approaching the car, handing her a claim ticket.

Rodney came close to her, his cigarette scent filling her nostrils. "Do anything, and this guy is the first to die. Then I'll take out his coworkers."

She walked into the hotel.

"What do you have against free clinics?" she asked as they waited for the elevator.

"Shut up," he said.

"Did you kill Clare?"

His mouth tightened. "You two would have been friends. You're exactly alike."

"Stubborn?"

"Too selfish to do anything for the greater good."

"Stopping a free children's clinic in Sonoma is for the greater good?"

"Free clinics are open graves," he replied curtly. The elevator doors opened. "Get in."

As they rose to the top floor, he fingered his belt. Would he kill her the same way he killed Phillip, with his belt? Why not just kill her in her car?

Maybe because he needed to hide her body, to give him time to get away before she was found. Maybe he needed something in his hotel room.

She then remembered something he'd said during the video chat. She now knew his story about Phillip trying to run him down in Miami was false, but he'd said he had noticed her talking to Phillip at the Zoe banquet, which indicated he already knew Phillip before the banquet. So why hadn't Phillip recognized him in the photos? "Was Phillip your friend?"

He snorted. "He was convenient."

"Convenient?"

"How often do you find a man who's friends with the girl you're going to kill, who looks exactly like you?"

So he'd chosen Phillip because he was Clare's friend. "You bought a duster on purpose. You wanted to pin it on Phillip on purpose."

He didn't answer her. She didn't need an answer. Clare had probably just let him into her townhouse, thinking he was Phillip.

"You can't pin my death on Phillip," she said.

"I was going to take your boyfriend, too, and pin it on him, but he wasn't with you when I walked into the spa. Bad luck, I guess."

Shaun. She'd never see Shaun again.

"I should thank Phillip," Rodney said. "If I hadn't seen him talking to you at the Zoe banquet, I would never have chatted with you." The elevator doors opened. "We're in the Grand Suite, darling."

As they walked down the hallway, the door to the Honeymoon Suite opened and a couple exited.

"Hi," Rodney said with a smile and a glance at Monica. She read his look clearly—*Do anything and they die.*

The couple walked past them and stood waiting for the elevator.

He let her into his suite, which had a wide open receiving area with a sofa and chairs in a semicircle. Against the left wall was a fully stocked bar next to a closed door. He nodded at the sofa. "Sit."

There was space behind the sofa. He'd stand there and loop his belt over her head like he'd done with Phillip.

No. She wouldn't go down without a fight. She tried to breathe through her tight throat.

She dipped her head a little, trying to fake terror. How ironic. She *was* afraid—very afraid—but she had to make him think she was too afraid to think clearly, to do anything.

She sat.

She heard him behind her, moving slowly, maybe trying to move quietly so she wouldn't know exactly what he was doing. But she'd already seen him fingering his belt. He could control his facial expressions, but he couldn't control the rest of his body.

She was ready when she saw the blur of the belt loop in front of her eyes. She quickly raised her hand up to her face so that he caught her wrist, too, when he pulled the belt around her throat. The leather dug into her wrist bone painfully, shoving her hand into her cheek, but her hand kept the belt from closing off her trachea. She rose up on her feet as he hauled her backwards, and after bracing one foot, she shot her free elbow back toward his head.

It collided solidly with something. Maybe his nose.

The belt loosened. She fumbled to pull it from around her neck.

His arm reached forward. She looked down and saw his right hand about to grab at her waist, to pull her back toward him.

And then memory flashed. Shaun's hand reaching just like this, to grab her from behind.

She reached across her body to grab his wrist with her left hand. She slipped her right forearm under his to grab at her left arm, trapping his arm against her body. Before he could react to what she was doing, she hauled upward with her right forearm and pushed down with her left hand, squeezing her arms together.

His radius bone snapped.

Rodney howled and jerked his arm out of her hold.

She dove over the back of the sofa and propelled herself toward the door. Then she heard the sound of a gunshot and felt a red-hot poker stab into the back of her right thigh. She fell. She'd been shot. Her entire leg was on fire.

The door to the suite burst open. "Police!"

But suddenly Rodney grabbed her arm, hauled her backward. The jostling sent waves of pain up her leg, making her nauseous. He dragged her behind the bar.

"Come any closer and I'll shoot her!"

She suddenly felt the hard, warm steel of the gun tip pressing into her temple, and wondered if this was the day she was going to die.

Shaun rode with Detective Carter in his car. They squealed into the driveway of the Fontana and Shaun was out the door before they'd come to a halt.

He sprinted to the front desk, where the manager immediately recognized him. His welcoming smile died as she saw the look on Shaun's face.

"Is there a Rodney Lassiter here?"

The manager shoved the clerk aside and searched the computer himself. "No, I'm sorry, sir."

Of course he wouldn't use his name. What name would he use?

But then Shaun remembered something. The watch. The expensive sunglasses. Dropping the name of the Efken hotel in Miami. Staying in the Presidential Suite. Rodney liked flaunting his money, and he liked using it. He liked being in luxury.

"Who has the Grand Suite and the Honeymoon Suite?" Shaun demanded.

"Er... Honeymoon is Mr. and Mrs. Holt. Grand Suite is... Emmanuel Rodney."

Gotcha.

"Give me your master key," Shaun said, and the manager handed it over. He and the police headed to the elevators.

As they rode to the top floor, Shaun saw the layout of the floor in his mind. There were only two suites, both with spacious layouts and balconies. Both rooms had two doors in and out—the main front door, and another door into a short foyer that led to the second bedroom in the suite.

As they headed down the hallway toward the Grand Suite, the crack of a gunshot rang out.

Shaun's breath cracked in his lungs.

Monica.

He swiped the master key and stepped aside as the police burst through the door. He heard Rodney's shout, "Come any closer and I'll shoot her!"

She was still alive.

"It doesn't have to end this way," Detective Carter shouted into the room. "Come out from behind the bar with your hands above your head and no one will get hurt."

He was behind the bar. Right next to it was the master bedroom door. However, the second entrance door to the Grand Suite was on the other side of the suite.

But the master bedroom had a balcony, and the master balcony for the Honeymoon Suite was close—Shaun could climb over. His brother Brady had stupidly done it during his bachelor party, which they'd held in the two suites on this floor. Shaun never thought he'd be grateful for Brady's reckless streak.

He raced to the Honeymoon Suite door and let himself

in. Policemen followed him, and he motioned for them to be quiet.

He entered the bedroom swiftly but cautiously in case the Holts were inside, but no one was there. He opened the sliding glass door, and the stiff breeze from the Bay slammed into him.

"Sir." One of the policemen stripped the bed and rushed to the bathroom to wet the sheet, which was 100% Egyptian cotton—even stronger when wet. They wrapped the end of the sheet around his waist tightly.

Shaun slung his leg over the railing, balancing on the edge that thrust out. He was only six floors up in this wing of the hotel, but he didn't look down.

The distance between this balcony and the other one seemed a lot farther than he remembered.

Just do it.

He leaped toward the balcony railing, grabbing hold. One foot landed on the edge, the other slipped, but he fumbled and regained his foothold. He rolled over the edge of the railing, and he was safe. He untied the sheet at his waist and the policemen pulled the sheet back onto their balcony.

He suddenly realized that once he opened the sliding glass door, Lassiter might hear him, but he looked through the glass and saw that the master bedroom door was closed. Lassiter wouldn't hear anything.

He pulled on the door and it opened. He slithered through and closed it behind him quickly. As he cleared the balcony, he saw one of the policemen with the sheet tied around his waist prepared to jump across also.

He waited for the other man to enter the bedroom, then signaled for quiet. He slowly, painfully twisted the handle to the master bedroom door. It opened silently, any sounds masked by Detective Carter's voice and Lassiter's shouts into the main room of the suite.

Lassiter was on the floor behind the bar, his back toward Shaun. His right arm hung limp, while his left held his gun awkwardly, only loosely pointed toward Monica's figure crouched on the floor.

Shaun took one breath. Then he darted forward.

His left arm swept upward under Lassiter's gun hand. A shot fired into the ceiling. Shaun hooked his right arm under Lassiter's chin and grabbed his sleeve for leverage as he tightened a choke hold.

The police descended, dog-piling on Lassiter and pulling him from Shaun's hold. Shaun rolled away.

Then he was scrambling toward Monica, tangling himself in her arms, burying his face in her hair.

"I thought I lost you," he said hoarsely.

"I thought I'd never see you again," she said.

He squeezed, holding her tighter.

She pulled back and looked up into his face. "You saved me. You were the protector you're meant to be, and you saved me."

"I'll always protect you."

"I love you," she said.

He kissed her, filling his senses with her, drinking her in as if she was sweet nectar. He pressed his cheek against hers and whispered, "I love you."

FOURTEEN

The only thing good about a wheelchair, Monica decided, was that Shaun had to carry her up and down the stairs.

He gently set her into the wheelchair that sat parked at the foot of the stairs. The party was already underway on the back porch of the Grant home.

"I don't see why Dad needs an announcement party," Monica said. "We've all known for weeks he was going to hire your father as consultant for the Joy Luck Life hotel project."

"But the O'Neills like parties," Shaun said as he wheeled her to the back door. "So we're always making up excuses for one."

They entered the back porch, which was filled with Monica's family. Rachel and Edward were talking to Detective Carter and Aunt Becca. Monica's father sat in a chair, his walker nearby, chatting with Patrick O'Neill, while Shaun's younger brother Brady and his wife showed off their new baby to Naomi and her fiancé Devon.

Detective Carter saw them and gestured them over. "We discovered more about Rodney Lassiter from his father's ex-housekeeper. She mentioned that Rodney had a twin sister who died from complications with pneumonia in a free clinic when he was about eight years old."

"A free clinic? But Rodney's family is wealthy."

"Apparently they weren't always. His father started his luxury foods distribution company when Rodney was in his late teens. The housekeeper mentioned that she'd overheard Rodney's therapist talking to his parents."

Rodney's therapist apparently hadn't been able to help him with his grief.

"According to the therapist, Rodney blamed his sister's death on the fact they had to go to a free clinic to treat his sister, and in his mind, that's why she died. He hated free clinics with an irrational obsession."

Was stalking ever rational?

"Rodney was homeschooled and so he'd entered college a year early, but he took a year off after his sophomore year. That would put him in Sonoma and L.A. around the time Clare was stalked."

"Did you find any evidence about her death?" Monica asked.

The detective shook his head. "No, but we discovered he met Clare here in Sonoma through a girl named Angela, who became Clare's roommate in L.A. Angela had no idea Rodney was the one stalking Clare."

"So he took time off school and lived as a field worker in Sonoma so he could harass Clare?" Monica said.

"It enabled him to blend in and not be noticed. And then he followed her down to L.A. He met you at the Zoe banquet because his parents donate to Zoe International."

"So him meeting Clare and meeting me were pure chance?"

"Maybe. We don't really know. He's undergoing a psych evaluation."

"Monica, there you are." Patrick came up to greet her. "I wish Liam and Michael could have come," he said, referring to his other two sons. "This is a big day."

"It is?" Monica asked.

Patrick winked at her. "This is the first official day of my retirement."

She laughed.

Mr. Grant then tapped a spoon against his water glass and Evita circulated with drinks for them all. "I want to propose a toast," he said. "To the forthcoming Joy Luck Life Spa and Hotel."

"Cheers!" rang around the porch.

Monica was genuinely at peace with her decision to stay and work at her father's spa as resident nurse, but a small chord of regret sounded deep in her chest. She would have liked to build the free children's clinic—no longer out of a desire to make herself feel significant, but because she genuinely wanted to bring this service to Sonoma county.

Maybe someday.

Her father cleared his throat. "I also want to make an announcement." He looked around at them, and his eyes found hers. "Monica, a percentage of all the profits from the hotel will be going directly into your free children's clinic."

"My clinic? But…" She tried to clear the fuzziness in her shocked brain. "My clinic is canceled."

"I want you to continue with the project," her father said.

Was this really her father saying these things? After everything he'd said only a few weeks ago?

He continued, "Do you remember that package that arrived at the house for you a week ago? When I called you about it?"

When Rodney had walked into the spa. She had forgotten about the envelope.

"I opened it and found it was your business plan," he said.

The copy of the plan she'd asked her hospital administrator friend to send to her.

"I read it and was impressed. And shamed." He rose slowly

to his feet, using the walker to cross the porch to her. He reached out and took her hand. "I realize I've been selfish about wanting my own desires over your dreams. When you were taken, I realized I didn't want to waste time arguing with you over what I want you to do with your life."

He squeezed her hand. "I've offered Shaun the position as head of security of the hotel, but we can hire someone else to fill the resident nurse position. Unless you change your mind."

"I…I don't know what to say."

"Say thank you," her father groused at her as he turned away. "I'm amazed at what manners my kids have." But she heard the teasing in his voice.

She turned to Shaun, who sat down at a chair next to her. "Is it true? You're going to be head of security? Not apply to the Sonoma PD?"

He nodded. "My counselor also thought it would be a good idea if I didn't go back into law enforcement," he said. "And to be honest, I'm looking forward to working at the hotel. I've enjoyed the times I worked as a security consultant for a few hotels that hired my dad for help."

She had never told him about her fears, which seemed silly now after everything that had happened. But she'd tell him soon. And she'd tell him that if he wanted to join the police force again, she wouldn't try to dissuade him. After seeing him rush in to save her, she realized he was a born protector, and she wanted to support him to be who God had made him to be. Her fears about losing him were best left in God's hands.

He leaned in closer. "And I realized something very important."

"What?"

"I realized that rather than spending my time protecting others, I would rather spend my time protecting you."

She smiled as he kissed her.

* * * * *

Dear Reader,

Thank you for joining me once again for this trip to Sonoma, California! This tourist spot is still a small community at heart, where romance blooms even among old acquaintances.

Shaun's struggle in this book is very close to my own struggles with "letting go and letting God." I always think *I* have to be the one to fix things, to protect people (even from themselves), to make things right. But the truth is, God is King. God, not me. And it is God who will make all things right.

Also, the Zoe annual banquet is not real, but Zoe International is committed to rescuing children from human slavery around the world, and I love their ministry. Check them out at www.gozoe.org/.

I love to hear from readers! You can email me at camy@camytang.com or write to me at P.O. Box 23143, San Jose, CA 95123-3143. I blog about knitting, my dog, knitting, tea, knitting, my husband's coffee fixation, knitting, food—oh did I mention my knitting obsession?—at camysloft.blogspot.com/. I hope to see you all there!

Camy Tang

Questions for Discussion

1. Monica is a nurse who is trying to launch a free children's clinic. She's passionate about this project because she really sees the need for it in her community. What projects or issues are you passionate about?

2. Shaun is dealing with a painful episode in his past, and it has turned into a bitter inner wound. Can you relate to his pain? What should his friends and family have done for him? What should he have done for himself?

3. Monica's plans for the free children's clinic are threatened by a mysterious stalker who is trying to scare her into stopping her project. How did Monica deal with this obstacle? Can you understand why she did what she did? What could she have done better?

4. Monica's Aunt Becca is a strong Christian who is comfortable speaking about her faith. Can you relate to her or do you know someone like her? What is your own way of sharing your faith?

5. Monica feels very different from her sisters—she sees herself as the wild child, the black sheep of the family compared to dedicated Naomi and quiet Rachel. Can you relate to how she feels? If she were your friend, what would you say to her?

6. When Monica discovers the stalker is getting more violent and reaching out to more people around her, she feels helpless, violated and guilty. Have you been in a situation where things were completely out of your con-

trol and it seemed to be going from bad to worse? How did you feel? What did you do?

7. Monica wants to feel significant. She thinks that this clinic will make her feel significant to the world and to her father. What does she learn about herself and her Heavenly Father? How does that impact the choices she makes at the end?

8. Monica, a Christian for all her life, is upset at God because she can't understand why He wouldn't bless this free children's clinic she wants to start. Have you been in a situation where you questioned why God didn't intervene for something worthwhile? How did you respond? How should we respond?

9. As things get worse, Monica just tries harder to accomplish her goal and gain some sense of control over the situation and the stalker. Have you ever felt this way? How did you respond? What would you have done differently from Monica?

10. Shaun spent a lot of time and energy trying to prove that Phillip was the stalker. Have you ever been so single-mindedly stubborn about something? What should Shaun have done?

11. Phillip Bromley gave the flashdrive of photos to Monica and told her, "I wanted to do something that I would be really proud of." Can you relate to how he was feeling when he said that? Why do you think it had become so important to him after all his deception earlier?

12. Shaun's theme verse is Psalm 74:12: "But God is my King from long ago; he brings salvation on the earth." What does that verse mean for you?

INSPIRATIONAL

Wholesome romances that touch the heart and soul.

COMING NEXT MONTH
AVAILABLE FEBRUARY 14, 2012

DANGEROUS IMPOSTOR
Falsely Accused
Virginia Smith

THE ROOKIE'S ASSIGNMENT
Fitzgerald Bay
Valerie Hansen

PROTECTING THE PRINCESS
Reclaiming the Crown
Rachelle McCalla

SHATTERED IDENTITY
Sandra Robbins

Louisa Morgan loves being around children.
So when she has the opportunity to tutor bedridden Ellie,
she's determined to bring joy back into the motherless
girl's world. Can she also help Ellie's father open his
heart again? Read on for a sneak peek of

THE COWBOY FATHER

by Linda Ford,
available February 2012 from Love Inspired Historical.

Why had Louisa thought she could do this job? A bubble of self-pity whispered she was totally useless, but Louisa ignored it. She wasn't useless. She could help Ellie if the child allowed it.

Emmet walked her out, waiting until they were out of earshot to speak. "I sense you and Ellie are not getting along."

"Ellie has lost her freedom. On top of that, everything is new. Familiar things are gone. Her only defense is to exert what little independence she has left. I believe she will soon tire of it and find there are more enjoyable ways to pass the time."

He looked doubtful. Louisa feared he would tell her not to return. But after several seconds' consideration, he sighed heavily. "You're right about one thing. She's lost everything. She can hardly be blamed for feeling out of sorts."

"She hasn't lost everything, though." Her words were quiet, coming from a place full of certainty that Emmet was more than enough for this child. "She has you."

"She'll always have me. As long as I live." He clenched his fists. "And I fully intend to raise her in such a way that even if something happened to me, she would never feel like I was gone. I'd be in her thoughts and in her actions every day."

Peace filled Louisa. "Exactly what my father did."

Their gazes connected, forged a single thought about fathers and daughters…how each needed the other. How sweet the relationship was.

Louisa tipped her head away first. "I'll see you tomorrow."

Emmet nodded. "Until tomorrow then."

She climbed behind the wheel of their automobile and turned toward home. She admired Emmet's devotion to his child. It reminded her of the love her own father had lavished on Louisa and her sisters. Louisa smiled as fond memories of her father filled her thoughts. Ellie was a fortunate child to know such love.

Louisa understands what both father and daughter are going through. Will her compassion help them heal—and form a new family? Find out in
THE COWBOY FATHER
by Linda Ford, available February 14, 2012.

Love Inspired Books celebrates 15 years of inspirational romance in 2012! February puts the spotlight on Love Inspired Historical, with each book celebrating family and the special place it has in our hearts. Be sure to pick up all four Love Inspired Historical stories, available February 14, wherever books are sold.